M. C. Beaton is the author of the hugely successful Agatha Raisin and Hamish Macbeth series, as well as a quartet of Edwardian murder mysteries featuring heroine Lady Rose Summer, various Regency romance series and a stand-alone murder mystery, *The Skeleton in the Closet* – all published by Constable & Robinson. She left a full-time career in journalism to turn to writing, and now divides her time between the Cotswolds and Paris. Visit www.agatharaisin.com for more, or follow M. C. Beaton on Twitter: @mc_beaton.

The Waverley Women series by M. C. Beaton

The First Rebellion
Silken Bonds
The Love Match

The Love Match

M. C. Beaton

Constable • London

CONSTABLE

First published by Crest, 1990

First electronic edition published 2011
by RosettaBooks LLC, New York

This edition first published in Great Britain in 2014 by Constable

Copyright © M. C. Beaton, 1990, 2011, 2014

The moral right of the author has been asserted.

A CIP catalogue record for this book
is available from the British Library.

ISBN: 978-1-47211-434-1 (A-format paperback)
ISBN 978-1-47210-157-0 (ebook)

Typeset i   Devon
Printe   YY

ONE

The large house in Hanover Square had a lost and abandoned look, as if no one lived there anymore. And yet servants could be seen going about their duties, and very occasionally a beautiful young lady would emerge and take the air accompanied by her maid.

The rooms seemed haunted by the voices of the bluestockings Mrs Waverley had invited to her soirées. But Mrs Waverley, that champion of rights for women, had betrayed her sex. She had married a colonel, now Baron Meldon, and had fled London. Society gossiped furiously after the announcement of the marriage and then forgot about her. They also forgot about her three adopted daughters, Fanny, Frederica, and Felicity. Fanny had married the Earl of Tredair; Frederica, Lord Harry Danger; and surely that third one had married as well.

But the third one, Felicity, was all alone. Mrs Waverley had gone, leaving her the house and a treasure in jewelry, enough to keep Felicity in comfort until the end of her days. But Felicity was an independent lady. She had sold her first novel and was already hard at work on another. The servants were all women, Mrs Waverley having never employed menservants, and the housekeeper, Mrs Ricketts, was always at hand to accompany Felicity should she care to go out. Felicity had recovered from the blow of Mrs Waverley's desertion of her, from the feeling of aching loss at being abandoned by her 'sisters'. But she had quarreled with Fanny and had tried to break up Frederica's marriage – sure Lord Harry did not mean to marry her – so they could hardly be expected to want to see her again.

In fact, she would have considered herself content had it not been for that ongoing nagging curiosity about her birth. Mrs Waverley had adopted the three girls from an orphanage. Both Fanny and Frederica and their then suitors had tried to find out why Mrs Waverley had chosen them, why they had initially been kept at an orphanage that demanded high fees from the relatives of the orphaned, yet in their case there did not seem to be any relatives, and why Mrs Waverley turned faint every time she saw the Prince Regent: Each time the girls had come up against a blank wall.

Of the three girls, Felicity had been the one who had most rigidly followed Mrs Waverley's training. Women were little better than slaves, and marriage was a way of selling themselves into bondage. But now that Felicity was independently wealthy and had a profession, she found her nights plagued by romantic dreams. The Season was beginning again. The air was full of excitement as if throbbing with all the hopes and dreams of the young misses arriving by the carriageload to look for husbands.

She was not vain, but her looking glass told her she was beautiful. She had masses of chestnut hair, an elegant figure, a sweet face, and large hazel eyes. Fanny was still abroad, Frederica was also on the Continent, and there were occasionally reports in the papers of their happiness and beauty. Although Felicity did not yet know it, her determination to remain a spinster was already crumbling.

Yet still she often toyed with the idea of taking up the reforming process where the treacherous Mrs Waverley had left off – at finding women who needed to be trained to educational independence. But women, thought Felicity bitterly, were all fickle. A man had only to smile on them and they forgot all their principles.

Mr Harvey, the bookseller who was publishing Felicity's book, had cleverly spread gossip about it through society before publication. It was called *The Love Match* by a Lady of Quality. The heroine was a rake who broke men's hearts and left them weeping. Mr Harvey was sure of its success.

So good was his promotion that by the end of the first day of publication every copy had sold out.

Felicity was sitting in her drawing room one day, admiring the handsome volume for the hundredth time, when Lady Artemis Verity was announced.

She put down the book and rose reluctantly to greet this unwelcome caller. Lady Artemis lived on the other side of Hanover Square and had recently returned from Italy. She was a dashing widow who had been engaged to a Mr Fordyce but had broken the engagement and run away from him. Her fine eyes were snapping with curiosity as she came into the room.

'I could not believe my ears, dear Miss Waverley,' she cried, 'when I learned Mrs Waverley had become married.' Lady Artemis giggled. 'So much for all her theorizing and prosing on about the independence of women. And Frederica! Now Lady Harry Danger, I believe. Tra la. You bluestockings seem to know how to snatch the best husbands from the marriage mart. So how do you go on? Never say you are living here alone.'

'No,' lied Felicity, although she did not know quite why she lied. 'My aunt is chaperoning me. A Miss Callow.'

'Indeed! I should like to make her acquaintance.'

'She is very old and frail and is lying down at the moment.'

'You must bring her to tea.' Her eye fell on Felicity's book. 'I see you have been reading *The Love Match*. A sad sham.'

'How so?' demanded Felicity angrily.

'Oh, everyone is tut-tutting over it and saying what a monstrous rake the authoress must be herself, but, my dear, I could swear it was all the imaginings of a virgin.'

'I found it highly convincing,' said Felicity stiffly.

'Well, you *would*, would you not?' Lady Artemis laughed. 'But to any woman of the world . . . la, the ravings of an innocent. Men do not fall in love with such a philanderer. If she is still in prime condition, they get their lawyers to offer her a sum for her favors. If she is past it, then a shilling and a glass of rum is the usual fee.'

'It is selling very well,' pointed out Felicity.

'A novelty. But society will soon become wise to her, and her next book will be left on the shelves. I have not seen you about. Are you determined to keep to Mrs Waverley's teachings and stay hidden from the world of men?'

'I have been busy of late,' said Felicity. 'But we shall no doubt meet soon.'

'I look forward to meeting your aunt. Miss Callow, is it not?'

'Yes.'

'Strange. I did not think you had any relatives . . . er . . . that you knew of.'

'Well, I have,' snapped Felicity.

She was still smoldering when Lady Artemis left. She picked up her book and scanned the pages. A blush mounted to her cheeks. Was it so naive? Was Lady Artemis being malicious? But, then, Lady Artemis could not know that she, Felicity, had written that book. Felicity bit her lip. Perhaps it was naive. How could she enlarge her experience? She could not attend balls and parties unchaperoned. She rang the bell.

Mrs Ricketts, a tall, powerful woman, came in and stood with her hands folded.

'I have been thinking, Mrs Ricketts,' said Felicity, 'that it is time I made my debut.'

'You cannot do that on your own, miss,' said Mrs Ricketts. 'Perhaps you had best advertise for some genteel lady to chaperone you.'

'I don't want a stranger in my house interfering with my ways and my independence,' said Felicity. 'Why do not we dress you up finely, Mrs Ricketts, and you can come with me?'

The housekeeper recoiled in horror. 'I couldn't do it, miss, and that's a fact, me with my plain speech and plain ways. Me sit with them dowagers? Your social standing would be in ruins. Besides, you don't get no invitations, and you won't get none neither, not without some older lady to nurse the ground.'

'Drat!' Felicity chewed her fingernails. 'Never mind, Mrs Ricketts, I shall hit on something.'

To her surprise, she had another caller that day, the famous actress Caroline James. Caroline had entered the Waverley household the year before in the guise of Lord Harry Danger's sister, Lord Harry having employed her to befriend Frederica and so further his suit. Caroline had, furthermore, been engaged to be married to Colonel James Bridie, now Baron Meldon, he who had run off with Mrs Waverley. The famous actress was a handsome woman and had conceived an admiration for the strong-willed Felicity.

'I put off coming to see you,' said Caroline, 'for actresses are not at all respectable, but a rumor reached me that you had been left alone, and I was anxious to reassure myself the world went well with you.'

'Yes,' said Felicity. 'I am truly independent now. Mrs Waverley left me this house and all the jewelry.'

'Then you are indeed fortunate,' said Caroline. The Waverley jewels were famous.

Felicity looked uneasily at her book, then said impulsively, 'I wish to confide in you, Miss James. Have you read *The Love Match*?'

'Not yet,' said Caroline, 'but all London is talking about it.'

'I wrote it,' said Felicity, coloring slightly.

'How clever of you!' exclaimed Caroline.

'I felt until today it was indeed clever of me,' said Felicity. 'But a certain Lady Artemis called on me. She is a widow and very *mondaine*. She does not know I wrote it, of course, but she sneered and said it was obviously written by a virgin, that it was naive. The heroine in my book is a rake, or rakess, if there is such a thing. I wish to enlarge my horizons and go about in society. I told Lady Artemis I was chaperoned by an aunt, a Miss Callow, but Miss Callow does not exist.'

'Then you must advertise for someone to take you about,' said Caroline, unconsciously echoing Mrs Ricketts.

'I don't want that,' said Felicity fiercely. 'I do not want to be under anyone's thumb again. Could *you*, my dear Miss James, not pretend to be Miss Callow?'

Caroline shook her head. 'I have too many performances, too many rehearsals.'

7

Felicity fell silent, and Caroline's blue eyes watched her sympathetically.

'Could you not,' said Felicity, raising her eyes, 'make me up to look like an elderly lady?'

'I could. But someone so young as yourself would not stand close scrutiny. What is your plan?'

'Oh, Miss James, if you could make me up to look like a dowager, I could entertain the ladies of the ton to prepare my own debut.'

Caroline looked amused. 'But when you are invited to a ball or party, you will be expected to arrive with this Miss Callow. You cannot split yourself in half.'

'I shall worry about that when the time comes,' said Felicity. 'Please say you will do this for me.'

Caroline hesitated, looking at the glowing, pleading face turned to her own. 'You could come with me to the theater,' she said, 'and we could try something.'

Felicity clapped her hands with delight. 'Now!' she said. 'Let's go now!'

The Marquess of Darkwater was strolling across Hanover Square when he saw Miss Felicity Waverley emerge with Miss Caroline James.

'What is that minx up to now?' he mused, watching as both ladies climbed into a carriage and drove off.

For the marquess not only knew who Felicity was but that she was the authoress of *The Love Match*. He had been present at the bookseller's when Felicity had first presented her manuscript and, unknown to her, had followed her home to find out who she was.

The marquess looked like one of the villains in Felicity's book. He was tall and tanned, with a broad-shouldered athlete's body. He had thick raven-black hair and piercing gray eyes. All Felicity's villains were handsome. The hero was plain-featured to show the readers that beauty of soul was more attractive to the rakish heroine in the long run than mere good looks. The marquess had returned from the West Indies the year before, where he owned sugar plantations. He was in his thirties and had been married to a delicate lady who had only survived the climate of the West Indies a few months before falling sick and dying. He had had some vague hope of finding a new wife in London, someone strong and brave enough to travel back with him to the plantations. But so far he had not met anyone to excite his interest . . . except, perhaps, Felicity Waverley, whom he considered highly unmarriageable in view of her spicy book. Unlike Lady Artemis, the marquess thought Felicity had a great deal of experience that no young lady should have in order to write such a shocking book, not knowing that the more purple passages of Felicity's prose had been culled from Greek and Roman classics.

He had hoped to meet Felicity at some society function, but it appeared Miss Waverley did not go out.

He went on his way but had only gone a few yards when he was hailed by one of his friends, Lord Freddy Knox. 'Are you coming to our ball?'

'Of course.' The marquess smiled. Lord Freddy had recently become married at the great age of nineteen to an heiress one year younger. The ball was to be the couple's first social engagement since their marriage.

'Good,' said Lord Freddy. 'I do hope it will be a success. Cassandra can barely sleep a wink with nerves.' Cassandra was his new wife, whose looks did not live up to her name, as she was small and plump and fair and vague, forever losing things and forgetting things. 'Any fair charmer we can ask for you?' demanded Lord Freddy.

'No,' began the marquess, and then his eye fell on the Waverley house. 'Well, there might be.'

'Only name her,' cried Lord Freddy.

'Miss Felicity Waverley. She lives over there.'

'I thought they were all married.'

'No, I believe Miss Felicity is still unwed.'

'There was a story going about,' said Lord Freddy awkwardly, 'that the three girls were foundlings and bastards adopted by Mrs Waverley.'

'And yet such lack of parentage did not stop either Tredair or Danger from marrying,' pointed out the marquess.

'True. If you want her, you shall have her. But this Miss Felicity might think it odd to receive a card at this late date. The ball's on Friday, and this is Monday.'

'Try,' said the marquess.

'Oh, very well, although I don't think my Cassandra will like it.'

Felicity sat in Caroline's dressing room. 'I will need to try to effect this transformation myself,' said Caroline, 'for no one else must be in on the secret. Now, let me see. I think a rather nasty birthmark might answer.'

'Why?' demanded Felicity. 'I want to be a sweet

white-haired old lady who will be doted on by the dowagers.'

'Because if you have a disfiguring mark on your face, then people will not look too closely. Before I even begin on your appearance, you must learn to move and walk like an old lady.'

The day wore on as Felicity went through 'rehearsal' after 'rehearsal' until she began to feel very weak and old indeed. Caroline then drew out wigs and makeup and white wax and got to work.

'You must always sit in a bad light,' she said at last. 'I have finished. You can look now.'

She held up a branch of candles, and Felicity looked in the mirror.

A white-haired old lady stared back. A purple birthmark disfigured her left cheek, and white wax wrinkles crisscrossed her brow. The huge wig shadowed her face. 'Never be seen without gloves,' said Caroline, 'or your hands will give you away. Do not sit too near the fire, or your wrinkles will melt. Now you will need to have all that taken off and then learn to put everything on yourself. It is a good thing Monday is the one night I do not have a performance.'

'Surely you don't perform on Sunday.'

'I rehearse. But don't tell anyone or they will close down the theater!'

At long last, Caroline pronounced herself satisfied. Then she said, 'Before you embark on this mad scheme, I trust you are only going into society to *observe*. You may feel Mrs Waverley betrayed you, but her principles were sound. It is a good thing for a woman to have her independence. It was you yourself who convinced me I should not marry.'

'And you are happy?'

'Yes, I am very happy. My success is secure; I am thrifty; I shall have enough money to keep me comfortably in my old age.'

Felicity looked again in the mirror. 'This birthmark is quite repulsive,' she said.

'It will serve its purpose,' said Caroline. 'Wear some of those famous Waverley jewels. All will look at those rather than at your face.'

'I hate those jewels,' said Felicity fiercely. 'Mrs Waverley enjoyed forcing us to wear them to excite the envy of the ton. I used to feel like some pasha's favorite. Fanny and Frederica must have hated them as well, for they left theirs behind. But if you think it will serve the purpose, I shall wear something dazzling.'

Felicity returned home late, feeling weary. Mrs Ricketts handed her a letter she said had been delivered that evening by hand. When she opened it, Felicity found a heavily embossed invitation card and a letter from Lady Freddy Knox. In it, Lady Freddy apologized for the lateness of the invitation, saying it had been dropped down the back of her desk by mistake.

'My first ball this Season,' said Felicity with satisfaction. 'I shall pen an acceptance.'

'You cannot go, miss,' pointed out Mrs Ricketts. 'You don't have a chaperone.'

'I have now,' said Felicity cheerfully, and told the appalled housekeeper of her plan.

In vain did Mrs Ricketts argue and protest. Felicity was determined to go. She would accept for herself and her 'aunt'; she would arrive alone and, on reaching the ballroom, say that her aunt was right behind her. She would make her entrance with a crowd of other people.

Mrs Ricketts at last threw up her hands in despair. She resigned herself to the inevitable. Felicity would be found out, and there would be a minor scandal. Her hopes of a debut would be dashed, but at least the household could return to peace and quiet.

Felicity was glad of the invitation, for it meant she could put off playing the part of Miss Callow in society for another week.

But she had a longing to try out her masquerade on someone first, just to see if it worked. Then she thought of Lady Artemis Verity and sent a servant across the square the next day with a card in which Miss Callow requested the pleasure of Lady Artemis's company.

At one point, she thought she would not be ready in time. The whole putting on of makeup, wig, and wrinkles took much longer than she had remembered. She instructed the grumbling housekeeper to half pull the curtains in the drawing room closed and to tell the other servants they would receive instant dismissal if they so much as breathed a word of what was going on.

Lady Artemis arrived at four o'clock in the afternoon, her fine eyes sparkling with curiosity. She was ushered into the shadowy drawing room.

'Pray forgive me for not rising to greet you, Lady

Artemis,' said a frail voice from a wing chair by the fireplace.

Lady Artemis walked forward and made her curtsy. She looked at the little old lady sitting in the chair and then averted her eyes quickly from that ugly birthmark and looked at the glittering diamond brooch pinned on her gown instead.

'Where is your niece, Miss Callow?' she asked, looking around.

'She has contracted a chill,' said Felicity, 'and is lying down. She sends her compliments and begs to be excused.'

'Poor thing,' said Lady Artemis. 'It is hard to believe such a strong character as Miss Felicity should succumb to anything. Are you but lately come to town, ma'am?'

'Yes, my lady.'

'A great surprise. Mrs Waverley led society to believe her girls had no relatives whatsoever.'

'Maria Waverley is a sad and devious woman,' croaked Felicity. 'She lied to suit what ends I do not know. The girls are in fact sisters of the name of Bride.'

'Indeed? Which county?'

'The Somerset Brides.'

'Never heard of them.'

'My lady, your manner distresses me. But, ah, then, the younger generation is mannerless to a fault,' said Felicity gleefully.

'Oh, I am sorry, Miss Callow. What you must think of me! But to more cheerful topics. Does your presence in London mean that Miss Felicity will be able to make her debut like a regular debutante? Poor Fanny and Frederica had to be courted on the sly.'

'Yes, I plan to take her everywhere,' said Felicity, 'my health permitting, of course.'

Mrs Ricketts brought in the tea things and stood about nervously until Felicity ordered her from the room.

'Tell me, Lady Artemis,' asked Felicity, 'why it was that your engagement to Mr Fordyce came to naught?'

'You are well informed,' said Lady Artemis with a little laugh. 'I found I had made a mistake.'

'In what way?'

'I simply felt we should not suit.'

Her curiosity almost made Felicity forget her role of old lady. 'Was his annual income not large enough?'

Lady Artemis put her teacup down in the saucer with an angry little click. 'Miss Callow! I am a very rich woman. I do not need to marry a man for his money.'

'I am sorry,' said Felicity. 'But, you see, love does not appear to enter into a society marriage.'

'Be assured,' said Lady Artemis dryly, 'that it most certainly entered into the marriages of both Miss Fanny and Miss Frederica Waverley.'

'If I could only be sure of that,' said Felicity half to herself.

She leaned forward and picked up her own book with one gloved hand. 'You told my niece that this was the work of a virgin, that the authoress had obviously no experience of the opposite sex.'

'Yes, that is my opinion.'

'You having, on the other hand, a great deal of experience?' said Felicity, enjoying all the license of being an old lady to the hilt.

Lady Artemis thought of her sexual antics with the ever-inventive Mr Fordyce and blushed and then rallied. This old lady could not know of such goings-on.

'I am a widow,' she said.

'Oh, yes, of course, that must help,' mused Felicity. 'But how do you suppose this writer could gain experience without . . . er . . . losing her virginity?'

Lady Artemis's eyes perceptibly sharpened, and Felicity raised her fan to her face. Ladies of the ton did not talk about virginity, especially elderly ladies of the ton.

'I suppose she must be content to observe, but that is hardly a substitute for firsthand experience,' said Lady Artemis. 'Tell me, Miss Callow, do you share Mrs Waverley's views? Or rather, as we must now assume, the views Mrs Waverley pretended to have?'

'I believe all ladies should be as highly educated as men,' said Felicity, 'and I believe more professional jobs should be open to them. Do you plan to marry again, Lady Artemis? You must forgive the curiosity of an old woman.'

'Perhaps . . . if I find someone to please me. I am fortunate in being able to pick and choose.'

'For Felicity's sake,' pursued Felicity, 'I must find out the marriageable, the eligible, men. Who is the top prize?'

'The Marquess of Darkwater,' said Lady Artemis promptly. 'But there is a drawback there.'

'Which is . . . ?'

'He is a widower, handsome and rich, but any bride of his would have to travel back to those wretched plantations in the West Indies with him. The climate killed his first wife. She wrote to a friend of mine when she first arrived, complaining about the heat and flies and the dreadful provincialism of the other plantation owners. Do you know some of them adopt American manners and the ladies do not sit down to dinner with the men? She was vastly shocked that Darkwater did not keep slaves but freed all the Africans and paid them wages.'

'Oh, excellent man!' cried Felicity.

'You do hold radical views, do you not? But of course there are many who are convinced that were they to wed Darkwater then they might persuade him to stay in England and send out an overseer.'

Felicity looked at her speculatively. 'And are you one of the hopeful, Lady Artemis?'

'La! I have not even met the man . . . yet. But he is a great friend of young Lord Freddy Knox, and so we are all sure of seeing him at the ball to be held by the Knoxes.'

'Felicity has been invited.'

'Indeed! Then it is fortunate for us other ladies that she holds such strong views on the rights for women. Nothing disaffects a man more.'

Felicity stiffened. 'And yet, Lady Artemis, Felicity led me to believe you shared her views.'

'For a time, for a time. But, la, one wishes the gentlemen to adore one, after all.'

'Like the Earl of Tredair, say? But, alas, he *did* marry Fanny without being the least bit put off by her principles.'

'My dear Miss Callow, Fanny Waverley was very beautiful, as I recall.'

'As is my Felicity,' said Felicity, thinking that being one's own aunt had great advantages. For example one could sit and praise oneself all one liked.

Lady Artemis rose to leave. She heartily wished she had not mentioned Darkwater's name. What if that minx Felicity should steal him away? Somehow she must contrive to see him before that ball and poison his mind against Felicity.

'Again I must beg you to forgive me for not rising,' said Felicity.

'Are you sure you are strong enough, ma'am, to face the rigors of a Season?' asked Lady Artemis, looking down at the huddled figure in the chair.

'I shall manage very well,' said Felicity. 'It is my wish to see Felicity married.'

'I thought Miss Felicity was against the idea of marriage.'

So she is, thought Felicity, but I am not telling *you* that, or it would be all about London. Aloud, she said, 'She is not against marriage, only against marriages of convenience, which, as she is very rich, she does not need to make.'

Lady Artemis discovered that the marquess had rented a house in Green Street. The next day, she made her way there, followed by her long-suffering maid, and walked up and down until she saw him appear, or rather she saw a richly dressed man appear and assumed it must be the marquess. As she came abreast of him, she stumbled and let out a scream. He raised his hat. 'Have you hurt yourself, ma'am?' he asked politely.

'A little twist, that is all,' said Lady Artemis. She smiled up at him. 'May I present myself. I am Lady Artemis Verity and you, I believe, are the Marquess of Darkwater.'

'At your service, my lady.'

'Oh, if you could just give me your arm to the end of the street,' said Lady Artemis, taking him literally. 'My poor ankle hurts a little.'

He offered his arm, and she leaned on it. 'I believe you attend the Knoxes' ball, my lord?'

'Yes. Will you be there?'

'Of course I shall.' She dimpled up at him. 'May I hope for a dance?'

The gray eyes looking down at her turned a trifle frosty and he said 'Certainly,' but she realized dismally she had appeared too bold.

'I shall not keep you to it,' she said. 'I was only funning. There are many pretty young ladies looking forward to the pleasure of your company.'

'I am sure none prettier than yourself,' he said gallantly.

'Oh, but London is evidently to have a new belle. Miss Felicity Waverley is emerging from seclusion.'

'Ah, yes, I have heard of her.'

'Quite farouche,' said Lady Artemis with a little

laugh. 'She holds strong views on the rights of women, yet she plans to marry some complaisant man and bend him to her ways.'

'Then I wish her every success.'

'Miss Waverley will no doubt be very successful. She pretends to appear helpless and feminine, but she is made of iron.'

'I gather you do not like Miss Felicity Waverley.'

'I?' Lady Artemis opened her eyes to their widest. 'I admire her immensely. So strong, so ruthless, so cynical.'

'We are now at the end of the street,' he pointed out.

'So we are,' she said gaily. '*À bientôt*, my lord.'

She stood and watched him walk away. Such shoulders! Such legs! Really, the prospect of living in the West Indies seemed more attractive by the minute.

TWO

Felicity was carried along on a wave of elation right up until half an hour before she was due to leave for the ball. Then the full enormity of what she was about to do struck her. Surely she would never get away with it!

She longed for the company of either Frederica or Fanny. Why had she quarreled with Fanny? Why had she been so stupid as to try to ruin Frederica's chances of marriage? Mrs Ricketts's doom-laden face was no help.

Nervously Felicity checked her appearance in the looking glass again. She was wearing a gown of fine white India muslin with an overdress of gold gauze fastened with pearl and gold clasps. A rope of fine pearls glowed against the whiteness of her neck, and she wore a little pearl tiara in her curled and pomaded hair. Her face was surely a trifle too pale. She reached for the rouge pot and then decided against it.

Oh, if only there were a real Miss Callow! For a brief moment, Felicity toyed with the idea of sending a servant to say she was unable to attend. But Lady Artemis's criticism of her book still rankled. She had to find out more about the real world. She, Felicity, did not even know what it felt like to be kissed by a man. Perhaps in the interests of literature she ought to begin by encouraging some man to kiss her. But how did you get a man to kiss you and then reject him? The critics had said her book was amusing and shocking. If she told some man she had only encouraged his advances to further her experience so she might get to work properly on her next novel, she would create more of a scandal in society than Fanny or Frederica had ever done.

Mrs Ricketts entered to say the hired carriage was at the door. Mrs Waverley had employed only women servants and had hired a carriage from the livery stables as she needed it, that way avoiding having men in her employ. Felicity allowed Mrs Ricketts to put a swansdown-lined mantle about her shoulders. She picked up her reticule and fan.

The evening had begun.

As the carriage lurched forward through the crowded streets, Felicity wished she had ordered a sedan chair instead, although it was becoming increasingly hard to find one. The benefits of a chair were that you stepped into it in your own hall and were borne straight into the house you were visiting, and as the chairmen ran along the pavements, there was no danger of being stuck for hours in a press of carriages.

22

She was anxious to make her entrance and get it over with. The Knoxes' house was only a few streets away, but it was a social disgrace to arrive on foot. Her carriage lined up behind the other carriages in the street where the Knoxes lived.

At last it was her turn to alight. She hesitated a little on the pavement and looked up at the house. It consisted of four stories, but it was smaller than her own, not being double-fronted. It was not overwhelmingly imposing, and there were no liveried footmen lining the steps. She saw a large party about to go in and fell in behind them, following the ladies to a room at the side of the hall where they were to leave their wraps.

Felicity felt quite old. Another Season, another batch of fresh, hopeful faces up from the country. She left her cloak with a maid and then walked back out into the hall and up the narrow staircase. The ball was in progress on the first floor. Three rooms had been joined together by dint of removing the connecting double doors for the evening and taking out most of the furniture. Felicity presented her card to a footman and made her curtsy to Lord and Lady Freddy Knox. Lord Freddy was a genial-looking young man, and his small, plump wife seemed too nervous to wonder where this Miss Callow who was supposed to be escorting Felicity had got to.

Felicity passed through to the ballroom and began to edge around the floor to where she could see a free seat against the wall.

She sat down and looked about her. A few couples were dancing energetically in the small space provided. More people were arriving by the minute, and it looked as if there would soon be no room left for dancing.

And then she saw Lady Artemis. She was standing by the door talking to a tall, handsome man. As Felicity watched, he turned and looked full at her. She studied him curiously, wondering whether to cast him in the role of villain or hero.

Definitely villain, she decided. Here was no plain yet honest hero but rather a tall, commanding man in exquisite tailoring and with a haughty, arrogant air. His eyes were as cold as the North Sea. His face was lightly tanned. He said something to Lady Artemis, still keeping his eyes on Felicity. Lady Artemis made a little moue, shrugged, and then began to lead him forward.

They came up to where Felicity was sitting, and she rose at their approach. 'Miss Felicity,' cried Lady Artemis. 'Where is your aunt, Miss Callow?'

'Somewhere in the press,' lied Felicity. 'She recognized an old friend.'

'May I present the Marquess of Darkwater. Lord Darkwater, Miss Felicity Waverley.'

Felicity curtsied and the marquess bowed. 'Would you care for some refreshment, Miss Waverley?' he asked.

'That would be very welcome,' said Lady Artemis, quick to include herself in the invitation.

And then Felicity saw Mr Fordyce, Lady Artemis's ex-fiancé. He was standing in the doorway. He was a small man with neat features and a trim figure. Lady

Artemis's pansy brown eyes widened in alarm. 'I am sure I see Lady Dunster signaling to me,' she said, and quickly wove her way between the groups of onlookers and dancers to make her escape.

'Would you like me to present myself to Miss Callow first?' Felicity realized the marquess was asking.

'No, there is no need to bother her,' said Felicity. 'She is a very old lady and does not like to be troubled when there is no need.'

'Meaning that you have decided for yourself I am safe and respectable?'

'Meaning that, yes, I should like some refreshment and, no, I do not think it necessary to trouble my aunt.'

'Very well. Follow me and I will try to beat a path for us.'

The rooms were now crammed. Dancing couples were colliding with spectators. The sound of voices beat upon the air, and the rooms were suffocatingly hot. A morning room on the half landing between the ground and first floors had been set aside for refreshments. There was nowhere to sit down. Waiters who were supposed to be circulating among the guests with glasses of wine, negus, champagne, and lemonade stood helpless, trapped in the press, their trays of drinks held high above their heads. The marquess, benefiting from his height, lifted two glasses from a tray and said to Felicity, 'Out again, I think. There must be somewhere we can find space.'

He led the way downstairs and paused on the bottom step. 'I suggest we be unconventional and sit on the stairs, Miss Felicity. Or would you rather stand?'

'No, I am quite happy to sit down,' said Felicity. She sat on a corner of the stair, and he sat close beside her to leave room for the guests who were ascending and descending. 'I do not know what is in these glasses,' he said, handing her one, 'but it looks like canary.' He took a small sip. 'Yes, it is, and not bad at all.'

'It is not at all like a ball,' ventured Felicity. 'I spent all day wondering whether I would remember the steps of the waltz, but I fear I am not even going to be allowed to dance.'

'It is a sad crush, and the newspapers will hail it tomorrow as a success. Freddy was so afraid no one would come, he invited far too many people.' He looked down at Felicity, noticing the pureness of her skin and the delicate rise and fall of her excellent bosom. It seemed amazing that such a pure and virginal-looking girl could ever have penned the words of *The Love Match*.

'I am led to believe you are a supporter of the rights of women,' he said.

'Yes, in a muddled kind of way,' said Felicity candidly. 'I am not much of a campaigner. Also, I have come to believe women only listen to such views when there is no hope of them being married. But the minute some gentleman appears on the horizon, they revert to simpering misses.'

'How very harsh. Most of them are not really simpering, you know. They are young and shy.'

'But it is a sad life when the sole aim of a gently born girl is to trap a husband.'

'Then why is the stern Miss Felicity Waverley appearing at such a frivolous event?'

'I weary of my own company.'

'You have Miss Callow.'

'Yes, but she is so very old, you see, that she cannot attend many functions or entertain much, so I am mostly on my own. Also, I like observing people.'

'Ah, yes. Taking notes. You do not write by any chance?'

'Not I,' lied Felicity. 'I enjoy reading. I thought that new novel *The Love Match* was very fine.'

'Well enough in its way,' he said, looking amused, 'but I should be frightened to meet the authoress. I would fear she would eat me alive.'

'I am sure she is a charming lady,' said Felicity. She took a sip of her wine and studied his mouth with interest. It was firm and well-shaped. She wondered what it would be like to be kissed by that mouth.

'My teeth are all my own,' he said in a mocking voice.

'I beg your pardon, my lord?'

'You were staring at my mouth.'

'Not I,' said Felicity. 'I was thinking of something else.'

'May I ask what you were thinking about?'

'Lord Darkwater!'

The marquess looked up. Lady Artemis, slightly flushed and out of breath, smiled down at him. 'You promised me a dance, my lord.'

'Did I? I really do not think there is any room left to dance, Lady Artemis.'

'Oh, but there is. You will excuse us, will you not, Miss Waverley?'

Felicity rose as well. 'Of course,' she said. She watched them mount the stairs together and wondered what to do. Then she found Mr Fordyce had joined her.

'Have you seen Lady Artemis?' he asked.

'Lady Artemis has just left with the Marquess of Darkwater. I believe they are going to try to dance.'

'What a good idea,' said Mr Fordyce. 'Will you do me the honor, Miss Waverley?'

'Thank you,' said Felicity.

They walked together up the stairs and then began to edge through tightly packed groups of people who were drinking or shouting to make themselves heard above the din.

'I do not think we should trouble to try to dance,' said Felicity. 'This is more like a rout than a ball.'

'No, no,' said Mr Fordyce eagerly, for he had just spotted Lady Artemis circling in the arms of the Marquess of Darkwater. He pulled her through a space in the crowd and onto the floor. Crammed in one corner a small orchestra was bravely playing away, occasionally hitting wrong notes when dancers collided with one of the players.

There were only three couples dancing. Felicity and Mr Fordyce made up the fourth. When they came abreast of Lady Artemis and the marquess, Mr Fordyce suddenly called, 'All change partners.' Lady Artemis and the marquess stopped dancing and looked at him in surprise. He quickly abandoned Felicity and seized Lady Artemis about the waist and forced her to move off with him. The marquess put his arm about Felicity. 'It seems you are left with me,' he said.

Couples dancing the waltz were supposed to dance twelve inches apart from one another, but the dancing space was so small Felicity found herself being crushed against the marquess. She tried to make the most of the experience. After all that was what she had come for – experience. So here she was, pressed tightly against a man. It was all very embarrassing. She felt hot and breathless. And then she very definitely felt a hand stroke her bottom. She jerked back, her face flaming. 'How dare you, sir!' she hissed.

'How dare I what?' asked the marquess crossly.

'You fondled my posterior.'

He looked startled and then smiled. 'Use your wits, Miss Waverley. I was holding one hand in mine and have the other firmly at your waist. Any one of the gentlemen behind you must have seen this crush as a delightful opportunity. Now, apologize.'

She looked at him, her lips trembling, for she had been badly shocked.

'Think, Miss Waverley,' he chided. 'I do not have three hands.'

'Oh, you are right,' said Felicity. 'I am sorry. But what a scandalous thing to do.'

He put his arm round her waist again. There was a scream from nearby them, followed by the sound of a slap. 'It seems as if the bold fellow has got his comeuppance,' murmured the marquess. He piloted her smoothly round the small space, noticing the party was beginning to get out of hand. People were drinking a great deal and becoming excited and bold with the proximity of so many bodies and the heat of the rooms.

Lord Freddy passed close to them, and the marquess said, 'If you do not let some fresh air in here soon, Freddy, your ball will become a romp.'

'Good idea,' said Lord Freddy. He walked toward the windows, and with the help of two footmen, raised both windows. A gale blew into the room; the candle flames streamed sideways and went out.

The ballroom was plunged into darkness. There was a little silence and then giggles and scuffles and screams.

The marquess put both arms around Felicity and held her tight. 'Stay still,' he said. 'Better I than some stranger.'

He could smell perfume from her hair, and he could feel her breasts pressed against his chest.

Felicity stayed very still, motionless, in his arms.

I believe she is frightened of me, thought the marquess. It's hard to think she wrote that book, but I was there when she delivered the manuscript. Could she possibly have been delivering it for someone else?

Lady Artemis, a little way away, was struggling in Mr Fordyce's crushing grip. 'Leave me alone,' she wailed.

'That is not what you used to cry when you lay naked in my arms,' he said fiercely. He forced his mouth against her own, ignoring her mumbled protests. Lady Artemis's mind was screaming that she would never more be trapped into performing Mr

Fordyce's degrading lustful exercises, yet her wanton body betrayed her and her lips grew soft against his own.

'You may release me now,' said Felicity crossly. 'The candles are being lit.'

He let her go a little, but kept one hand at her waist. Those normally cold eyes of his were lit with a mocking, teasing look. 'This ball is going to become very wild,' he said. 'Do you not think we should find your aunt and leave?'

Felicity looked about her, at the flushed faces and glittering eyes, and shook her head. It was too good an opportunity to observe society at its worst. She knew from gossip that this occasionally happened. Bound as they all were by the strict laws of conventions, by the many social taboos, occasionally the ton would rebel and kick up their heels. Glasses were being snatched off trays as soon as they appeared, and toasts were being drunk. Lady Artemis, Felicity noticed, was no longer dancing stiffly in Mr Fordyce's arms but was sinuously swaying. Both their faces were hot and flushed, and their lips looked swollen.

'I cannot stay with you all evening, even at such an affair as this,' said the marquess. 'It would occasion comment. Come. Let us find Miss Callow.'

'I will look for her myself,' said Felicity, and pulling free, she disappeared into the crowd. Lord Freddy hailed the marquess again. 'What am I to do?' he said. 'They will take the house apart.'

'Serve only lemonade,' said the marquess. 'That will soon cool their fever.'

Lord Freddy nodded and soon could be heard calling to the footmen.

Felicity was meanwhile deciding to make her escape. The press of people was too much and the noise of so many voices deafening.

And then a young man smiled down at her and said, 'May I help you, ma'am? You seem in need of protection.'

Felicity looked up into his face, and then smiled back. Here was the hero of her book. He had a square, plain face, a snub of a nose, clear blue eyes, and thick unruly fair hair. His figure was stocky, and his cravat was limp.

'Thank you,' said Felicity. 'I was on the point of leaving.'

'Then follow me and I will take you downstairs,' he said. 'Allow me to introduce myself. My name is Bernard Anderson.'

'And I am Felicity Waverley,' said Felicity. 'Do you really think you can get me out of here? There appears to be a solid wall of people between us and the stairs.'

'Follow me,' he said. He lunged at the crowd with such energy that people squeezed to either side to let him past, and Felicity quickly followed. She took a deep breath of relief once they had reached the comparative peace of the stairs.

'May I fetch your mother or your chaperone?' he asked.

'You are very kind,' said Felicity. 'But my aunt, Miss Callow, is an eccentric old lady, and I fear she has already left without me.'

'But you have a carriage?'

'Yes, thank you, Mr Anderson.'

'Then I shall escort you to it.'

As they stood on the step waiting for the carriage to be brought round, Felicity found herself very much at ease in Mr Anderson's company. He prattled on about what a sad crush it was and how Lord Freddy had commanded the waiters and footmen to serve nothing but lemonade, but had forgotten to tell his wife, who had promptly countermanded the orders.

When Felicity's carriage arrived, he begged leave to call on her and Miss Callow the following day. Felicity thought quickly. She would need to receive him as Miss Callow, but as Miss Callow she could sing her own praises. So she thanked him prettily and said she looked forward to seeing him.

Mr Anderson made his way back up the stairs, but before he reached the top he found himself confronted by his mother.

'What were you doing with Felicity Waverley?' demanded his mother. Mrs Anderson was a big, imposing woman with big, imposing breasts that were thrust up by her corset so much that her heavy bulldog chin appeared to be resting on them.

'I was escorting her to her carriage, Mother,' said Bernard mildly. 'I promised to call on her tomorrow.'

'You will do no such thing,' said Mrs Anderson. 'Those Waverley girls are foundlings and bastards. And there is no dowry there. For it is rumored Mrs Waverley ran off and left that one penniless.'

Bernard's face fell. 'She is awfully pretty,' he mumbled.

'But portionless,' said his mother. 'Come. We are going home. You know you must find an heiress, Bernard, yet you waste your time squiring the most unsuitable female at the ball!'

In her guise of Miss Callow, Felicity sat in her darkened drawing room the next day and waited for callers. Mr Anderson would come and she would see if she, as her own aunt, could get him to offer to take her 'niece' on a drive.

But the first person to arrive was the Marquess of Darkwater. Felicity shrank back in her winged armchair and asked to be excused for not getting up.

'I came to pay my respects to Miss Felicity,' said the marquess, sitting down opposite.

'I am afraid my niece is lying down,' said Felicity.

'A pity. Last night was a sad romp, was it not?'

'Quite disgraceful,' said Felicity sternly. 'I would not have believed the ton capable of such shocking behavior. Felicity told me there were many loose screws present.'

The marquess blinked and then said, 'I trust she spoke favorably of me.'

'She did not mention you at all,' said Felicity maliciously. 'But she did meet a most charming young man. A Mr Anderson.'

'Oh, yes?' said the marquess. 'I do not know him.'

'Well, you wouldn't. He is not *fast*.'

'What a low opinion you have of me and on such short acquaintance. Besides, it is ladies who are fast, not men.'

'Lady Artemis Verity,' announced Mrs Ricketts.

Lady Artemis sailed into the room, both hands outstretched in welcome. Felicity felt every bit like the grumpy old lady she was supposed to be. Lady Artemis was wearing a dashing bonnet and a high-waisted morning gown with long tight sleeves ending in pointed lace cuffs. Her face was glowing, and her lips were delicately rouged.

'My niece is resting,' said Felicity before Lady Artemis could speak.

'What is happening to these young girls, Lord Darkwater?' said Lady Artemis. 'No stamina.'

'That is true,' said Felicity. 'One obviously toughens up with age.'

Lady Artemis ignored her. Her eyes were fixed on the marquess. She began to talk about the ball, about the crush, and about how disgracefully everyone had behaved. The marquess replied pleasantly that at least the Knoxes had had their first success. Any affair where so many women fainted, so many coachmen fought outside for places, and so many gentlemen were carried out drunk was always deemed a success.

While he talked, Lady Artemis studied his handsome face. Here was a man who would make her an ideal husband. Not Mr Fordyce, who had managed to get into her bed after the ball and had left her feeling peculiarly degraded. She had had several affairs since her husband died. Now she craved respectability. She had tried her best to be discreet, but she knew there were many whispers about her.

She urged the marquess to talk about the West

Indies and listened to him eagerly, interrupting every now and then to say she longed to travel, to see such countries. Felicity sat hunched up in her chair behind her wrinkles, feeling forgotten.

At last the marquess rose to take his leave, and Lady Artemis rose as well. 'We shall all need to be on our best behavior now, Miss Callow,' said Lady Artemis. 'After that ball, you know. Society has shocked itself and will become very prim and proper for a while.'

'I shall tell Felicity of your call,' said Felicity.

After they had left, she sat and brooded. She was just about to rise and go up to her room, when to her surprise, Mrs Ricketts entered to say that a Mrs Anderson had called. 'I did not usher her up, miss, for she looks bad-tempered.'

'I shall see her,' decided Felicity. 'Draw the curtains a little more, Ricketts.'

Mrs Anderson had come to see Felicity for herself. She was alarmed because her son had turned peevish on the subject instead of being his usual malleable self. Mrs Anderson was a fairly rich woman in comfortable circumstances, but she was greedy and, being a doting mother, had an inflated idea of her son's attractions. Bernard should marry an heiress – on that she had her mind set.

She was startled to be told by the housekeeper that Miss Felicity was lying down but that her aunt, Miss Callow, would receive her. Now Bernard had mentioned the existence of this aunt, but Mrs Anderson had not believed such a creature existed. No one had noticed any chaperon with Felicity at the ball.

When she entered, she curtsied to the old lady in the chair. But at first Mrs Anderson's covetous eyes did not even notice that disfiguring birthmark. They had fastened on the old lady's jewels. Felicity was wearing fine kid gloves with rings worn over the gloves and heavy bracelets encrusted with jewels at her wrists. Six strands of the finest diamonds blazed at her neck. An oil lamp had been cleverly placed so that although Felicity's face was in shadow, the jewels caught fire and blazed with a wicked light.

Mrs Anderson gulped and sat down. 'Is Miss Felicity present?' she asked.

'No, Mrs Anderson,' said Felicity, taking an instant dislike to Bernard's mother. 'She is lying down. My niece is a delicate flower, Mrs Anderson, and was vastly shocked at the behavior of the guests last night.'

'As was my son,' said Mrs Anderson. 'He was fortunate enough to be of assistance to your niece.'

'So Felicity told me,' said Felicity. 'He was all that was kind and helpful.'

'Society does gossip so,' said Mrs Anderson with a false little laugh. 'I was led to believe poor Miss Felicity had been abandoned and was unchaperoned.'

'I am surprised you should listen to malicious gossip,' said Felicity sternly. 'Felicity is very well protected by me. She is plagued by fortune hunters . . . of course.'

'Of course,' said Mrs Anderson weakly, looking at those glittering jewels.

'Apart from her own wealth,' said Felicity, 'which is

considerable, she will, of course, inherit my fortune on my death.'

Mrs Anderson felt more wretched by the minute. Why had she not let Bernard call? She must make her escape and send him round immediately.

'Why did your son not come with you?' asked Felicity. She still thought kindly of Bernard but put his mother down as an avaricious, vulgar creature.

'He sent me . . . because he is very shy, don't you know . . . to get me to beg you to give him permission to take Miss Felicity on a little drive in the park. But she is not feeling at all the thing, so . . .'

'I am sure if he calls at five o'clock, my niece will be glad to take the air with him,' said Felicity.

Mrs Anderson beamed. 'I shall go and tell the poor boy immediately. To be frank with you, Miss Callow, I have never before seen him quite so taken with any lady.'

Felicity bowed her head in assent.

Mrs Anderson rose in a flurry of silk, anxious to take her leave.

As soon as she had gone, Felicity cast a worried look at the clock. Four o'clock! She must work hard or she would never manage to transform herself back into Miss Felicity Waverley in time.

At five o'clock, Mrs Ricketts was posted in the hall with instructions to tell Mr Anderson that Miss Callow was lying down, and then summon Felicity.

Felicity had been wondering whether Bernard was worth all the trouble. Surely such a mother must have passed on her greedy traits to her son. But when she saw him standing in the hall, looking shy and

38

awkward yet so very happy to see her, she was glad he had come.

They had a sedate drive in the park, Felicity carefully confining her conversation to observations on the people she saw and the inclemency of the English weather. Because of Bernard, Felicity began to contemplate the idea of marriage for the first time. Here was no man to bully her or enslave her, but a pleasant fellow who would allow her to run her own household. It would be a relief not to feel alone in the world. Of course, his mother was a problem, but Felicity felt sure she could easily put that lady in her place. It was the thought of the irregularity of her position, her lack of parents, her lack of support, that made Felicity feel quite weak. For the first time, she realized why even women of independent means finally crumbled and preferred to be married rather than to face the rest of their lives alone. At one point, the Marquess of Darkwater's face seemed to float in front of her eyes, his gaze searching and mocking.

But the marquess was a powerful and dominating personality. He would not allow her any freedom. Nor would such an aristocrat wish to ally his name to a girl with the background of a foundling hospital and orphanage. 'And yet,' said a treacherous voice in her head, 'both Fanny and Frederica managed to find men who did not care about their birth.'

Bernard was seeing Felicity Waverley as no one had seen her before, shy and grateful for each little attention and compliment.

Lady Artemis was driving round the square when

Felicity arrived home. She saw Bernard Anderson tenderly helping Felicity to alight and saw the warmth and admiration in the young man's face.

She felt a stab of pure jealousy. Those Waverley girls always managed to get men to fall in love with them. She would find out the name of that young man and see if she could draw his attention to herself. She had flirted with Darkwater, but he had remained cold and uninterested. She was only twenty-seven, but she felt much older. She had always been secure in the power of her beauty. It became important to her to prove she could take at least one man away from Felicity.

The Marquess of Darkwater was sitting in his club, wondering about Felicity Waverley. He could not get her out of his mind. She was an odd contradiction. Had she really written that book? Or had that ugly and sinister aunt of hers written it for her?

His mind turned to the aunt. Unlike Lady Artemis and Mrs Anderson, he had not been put off by the birthmark or dazzled by the jewels. She was remarkably like Felicity and with the same young, hazel eyes. Felicity had remarkable eyes, he mused, golden brown with green flecks. There was a nagging little suspicion about that aunt somewhere in his mind. He remembered the room, how it had been darkened and how the light had been carefully placed so as not to shine on Miss Callow's face. Like a theater scene.

He decided to call unexpectedly on the following day to find out who would receive him . . . Felicity or Miss Callow.

40

THREE

Felicity awoke the next day with a feeling of antici-
pation. She lay in bed, enjoying that rare sensation
and wondering dreamily what was causing it. Then
she remembered Bernard Anderson. She was looking
forward to seeing him again.

   She did not have any romantic thoughts about him.
Rather, she looked on him as a newfound friend. She
need not dress up as Miss Callow and call on the parents of eligibles. Bernard would court her and, yes, she
would very likely marry him and settle down to a con-
tented life. She would invite Frederica and Fanny to
the wedding and hope they had forgiven her. Perhaps
they had not been in love either, but had merely
wearied of the unnatural life they had been leading
under Mrs Waverley's protection. Should she ask Mrs
Waverley? Felicity's face hardened. Mrs Waverley
had not really cared for any of them. She had bought

herself a family out of an orphanage, and the minute a husband had appeared on the scene, she had forgotten all about them. But, Felicity mused, she had left the house and all the jewels. Yes, it would only be fair to ask Mrs Waverley.

She rose and dressed, ate a light breakfast, and sat down to work on the first chapter of her new novel. She had decided to use the same heroine, but her female rake had been left in the last book on the point of reform, and on the point of marrying her plain but honest hero. Clorinda, as the heroine was called, must now jilt the hero and continue her amorous adventures. Felicity needed a new villain. The Marquess of Darkwater's face rose before her mind. She began to write busily.

The day wore on, and when she looked up, it was three in the afternoon. With an exclamation, she dropped her pen and began to change into one of her finest morning gowns. Bernard would surely call. But no sooner had she dressed than Mrs Ricketts knocked at the door to say the Marquess of Darkwater was waiting in the hall.

Felicity bit her lip. She did not want to see him, but, on the other hand, he was now her villain and she should study him closely.

She opened the door and told Mrs Ricketts to show the marquess up to the drawing room. She was to say that Miss Callow was out on calls.

'You can't see him alone, miss,' said Mrs Ricketts severely.

'Oh, yes, I can,' retorted Felicity. 'Leave the door

of the drawing room open, and be on hand in case I want you.'

Felicity ran to the mirror and checked her appearance. Her gown of palmetto green satin with long sleeves and a Vandyke ruff looked rich and stately. Her hair was dressed high on her head with little tendrils being allowed to escape and fall round her cheeks.

The marquess rose at her entrance and bowed and said he was sorry not to have the pleasure of seeing Miss Callow.

'Why?' asked Felicity curiously.

He raised his thin black eyebrows. 'I find her a most interesting lady,' he said. His eyes were mocking, and Felicity wondered whether he had penetrated her disguise on his previous visit.

'I have just come from Harvey, the bookseller,' he went on. 'You said you had read that novel *The Love Match*. Harvey hopes to have a new book from the authoress shortly.'

Felicity feigned a yawn of boredom. 'I have little time to read these days, my lord.'

'But he told me a most interesting thing. It appears that perhaps our bold authoress gained her knowledge from Greek and Roman classics rather than from life, if you take my meaning.'

'No, I don't,' said Felicity rudely.

'It appears that instead of being the work of an experienced lady of the ton, it may instead be the work of a highly imaginative and well-educated innocent.'

'Unlike you,' said Felicity, 'I do not have the necessary experience to judge the book.'

'You surprise me.' He held up his hand as Felicity glared at him. 'I mean,' he went on smoothly, 'that Mrs Waverley had the reputation of being a great educator. 'Tis said you and the other two ladies were better educated than many men.'

'Perhaps,' said Felicity.

There came the sound of a carriage stopping outside. Felicity rose and hurried to the window. But it was not Bernard Anderson, only a young man who had stopped his carriage to talk to a passerby.

She returned to her seat, looking downcast. The Marquess of Darkwater realized with a little shock that Miss Felicity Waverley was most definitely not enjoying his company. In fact, she was clearly waiting and hoping for the arrival of someone else. It was a new experience for him. His title, his looks, and his fortune had always ensured that women looked on him with glowing admiration and hung on his every word.

'Perhaps you would care to accompany me on a drive tomorrow?' he found himself saying.

'No, that will not be possible,' replied Felicity firmly. 'I have other engagements, oh, not only for tomorrow but for weeks to come.'

The snub was obvious. He rose to take his leave. 'I am sure,' he said, 'Miss Callow would welcome a visit from me. Present my compliments and tell her I will call on her.'

'I do not think that is a good idea,' said Felicity.

'Why, I pray?'

'I regret to inform you, my lord, that Miss Callow

took you in dislike. You must forgive her. She is old and set in her ways and not likely to change her mind.'

He was suddenly very angry. Yet did not he himself firmly dismiss people he considered tiresome?

But he found his anger was so great he could barely take a civil leave of her.

At that moment, Bernard was sitting in the Green Saloon of his mother's house in Cavendish Square, and feeling miserable and awkward. He had been all set to go and call on Felicity with his mother's blessing but Lady Artemis Verity had come to call. Being a widow, Lady Artemis enjoyed the freedom of being able to call on Mrs Anderson on her own. A young miss would have had to be taken along by her mother or chaperone.

Mrs Anderson was flattered by the visit. She was even more excited when she noticed the melting glances Lady Artemis was throwing in the direction of Bernard. Mrs Anderson knew Lady Artemis was rich. Even better than that, she had a title and was well-established in the ton, unlike Felicity Waverley who was of doubtful birth and social standing to say the least.

And when Lady Artemis, with another flirtatious glance at Bernard, said she would be delighted if both mother and son would grace her box at the opera that evening, Mrs Anderson was already mentally preparing her son for his wedding.

Bernard was terrified of Lady Artemis. She was undoubtedly very pretty in the accepted mode. She had rich brown hair with glossy ringlets falling on either side of her face. Her complexion was fashionably pale, her pansy brown eyes large and sparkling, and her features piquant and delicately formed. But Bernard was twenty and Lady Artemis was twenty-seven, and she appeared to him a terrifyingly older and sophisticated woman. He longed for the fresh and undemanding company of Felicity Waverley.

As soon as she had taken her leave, Bernard rose to his feet. 'Where are you going?' demanded his mother.

'Thought I would call on Miss Waverley,' mumbled Bernard.

'Nonsense, my son. Lady Artemis is a catch, and did you mark how she looked at you? Forget Felicity Waverley. No breeding there and no title either.'

'But, Mother . . .'

'Do as you are told, Bernard!'

So, as usual, Bernard did what his mother told him.

After a week of isolation, Felicity would have welcomed a visit even from the uncomfortable Marquess of Darkwater. The London Season was well underway, yet she sat in the great house, ignored and alone.

She summoned up her courage, put on the disguise of Miss Callow, and went to call on one of Mrs Waverley's acquaintances, Lady Dexter, a lady who had claimed to share Mrs Waverley's radical views.

It took a great deal of courage to emerge into the daylight as Miss Callow, but Felicity felt it was the only way she could get invitations for herself and to find out what had happened to Bernard Anderson.

She was just about to go out when Mrs Ricketts came to say that Mr Fordyce had called.

'Tell him Felicity is resting and put him in the drawing room,' said Felicity, 'but tell him I am about to go on a call and can only spare him a few moments.'

Mr Fordyce got to his feet as the bent old lady came into the drawing room. 'Forgive me for disturbing you, Miss Callow,' he said. 'I was anxious to speak to Miss Waverley.'

Felicity walked forward leaning heavily on a stick and settled herself in the wing chair. 'What do you wish to speak to my niece about?' she asked.

'I knew Miss Felicity when I lived in the house next door and was engaged to Lady Artemis Verity,' said Mr Fordyce. 'I wondered, perhaps, if Miss Felicity saw much of Lady Artemis these days.'

'As little as possible,' said Felicity.

'But they were great friends at one time!' exclaimed Mr Fordyce.

'I believe at one time it amused Lady Artemis to pretend to share my niece's views on the rights of women,' said Felicity, 'but that was only a pretense.'

'You must not think ill of Lady Artemis,' said Mr Fordyce. 'She is a creature of nature.'

Felicity blinked. 'Like a wasp?'

'No, Miss Callow, like a pretty fluttering bird.'

'Dear me, Mr Fordyce. I would like to be of help to you, but your fluttering bird is not to be found here.'

'I do not understand what she is about,' said Mr

Fordyce wretchedly. 'Why she must needs seek out the company of that youth, Bernard Anderson, I do not know.'

'We do know Mr Anderson slightly,' said Felicity. She experienced a sinking feeling in her stomach. 'Is Lady Artemis enamored of him?'

'She cannot be, ma'am!' cried Mr Fordyce. 'What has a youth of his years to offer her?'

'Youth and kindness and a good heart,' said Felicity wistfully.

'I beg you, Miss Callow, if your niece has any inkling of how Lady Artemis feels toward me, I would be most grateful if she would let me know.'

Felicity bowed her head. 'Be assured, Mr Fordyce, my niece is not intimate with Lady Artemis. Now I beg you to excuse me. I have calls to make.'

So that was that, thought Felicity, as she climbed into her carriage. Faithless Bernard! Or was it that his greedy mother saw better game? For one moment, she contemplated canceling the call and returning to the house. Her book was barely started.

But the day was gray and cheerless and threatening rain, and the large house looked dark and gloomy. She climbed into the carriage and told the coachman to take her to Lady Dexter's.

'You have left the preparations for Felicity's Season a little late, Miss Callow,' said Lady Dexter after her odd visitor had been given tea. Really, this Miss Callow was extraordinary, covered as she was with blazing jewels. It was hard to look at her face, for one's eye kept being distracted by all those flashing rings and bracelets and brooches. Lady Dexter remembered the attempts to thieve the Waverley jewels and marveled at the old lady's courage in being seen abroad with such a king's ransom on her. 'I will see what I can do, Miss Callow,' she went on. 'Your visit is a great surprise, for Mrs Waverley put it about that her girls were orphans and had not any relatives.'

'Maria Waverley told a great deal of lies,' said Felicity. 'I do not like to see my Felicity suffer because of them.'

'Oh, I agree. Now, I am giving a musicale tomorrow night, Miss Callow. Not knowing of your existence, I did not send you a card, but I should be delighted if you and your niece would attend. Many eligibles will be coming. Who is new on the market? There is Darkwater. Then there is Mr Johnson. There is the divine Colonel Macdonald, but lately come to town to set all our hearts aflutter.'

'We should be pleased to come,' said Felicity, although wondering how she was to manage to arrive as Felicity and explain the absence of her aunt.

'Splendid. Now do not run away, Miss Callow, for I am expecting several ladies for tea, some of whom might prove useful to you.'

Felicity passed inspection by the ladies of the *ton* very creditably. The jewels were passport enough. Society had very strict social laws to keep upstarts at bay. Breeding was all. Vulgar money could not buy entrée. Or so they claimed. But the older and more

aristocratic the family, the more ruthless the determination to hold onto power and land. That was the
reason so many weeping girls were led to the altars
of London to marry old and diseased men. Girls
might weep, but they, like their parents, knew what
they owed their ancient names. Love could be found
outside marriage. There was only one commandment
there to obey – Thou Shalt Not Be Found Out. And
so the bartering went on: my ancient name for your
dowry. The ladies Felicity met that afternoon bowed
down before her display of jewels and pronounced her
a fascinating character.

The thieves who had originally tried to steal the
Waverley jewels had been transported, the highway-
man who had in turn tried to get them had been shot,
and the underworld of London still buzzed with occasional rumors, but no one dared try where others had
so disastrously failed.

But there was a new breed of villain on the London
scene: the confidence trickster. The wicked lord in the
novels Felicity and other ladies read who seduced and
betrayed and left some innocent weeping in the snow
with a baby in her arms existed in real life, but he
was not an aristocrat but a clever and ruthless man
masquerading as one. Society prided itself so much on
the great wall of strict taboos and shibboleths it had
built around itself to keep the unfashionables at bay,
that smug and secure, it was often betrayed by its own
greed. So as Felicity was able to masquerade as an old
lady by dint of attracting all eyes to her fabulous jewelry, so Colonel Macdonald was able to gain entrée to

the best houses because of his handsome face, charm of manner, and reputation of having gained a fortune from an Indian prince while commanding a sepoy regiment.

It was fashionable for military men to forget about wars and campaigns in civilian life. The bravest of soldiers often appeared as a dandy only interested in the cut of his coat or the folds of his cravat. Of course, they discussed serious matters together in their clubs, but Colonel Macdonald made sure he performed only in the company of the ladies, where such serious subjects were forbidden.

He had been born Angus Mackay, son of a Scottish weaver. He had served as a private in a Highland regiment in India and had deserted as soon as he saw that his regiment was to be posted to the Peninsular Wars. Before he deserted, he stole several items of regimental plate, which he sold in Glasgow. He had studied the manners and bearing of his senior officers. In Glasgow, he had become Mr Guy Flint, a Virginian tea merchant, and there had courted and married the daughter of a wealthy Scottish merchant. He had managed to spend her dowry very quickly on luxurious living and had taken himself off to fresh pastures right after his young bride had presented him with a son. He moved to the lake district the poets had made fashionable and had begun to court the daughter of a local landowner. Again, his suit was successful. He married her, but, again, her dowry, although generous, was not enough to keep him in the luxuries to which he had rapidly become accustomed. He deserted her and moved south. He was after bigger game. He took on the name and character of Colonel James Macdonald, Member of Parliament for Linlithgowshire. One would think that the very claim of being an M.P. would have exposed him, but Linlithgowshire was believed to be in Scotland, and Scotland was a world away, and society was used to Members of Parliament who represented odd and barbaric constituencies and who never put in an appearance at the House of Commons, and so he was socially accepted.

He was a fine-looking man with silver-blond hair, a Greek god profile, blue eyes, and a slight Irish accent, which fell most seductively on listening ears. He made a great joke of his accent, saying he belonged to the Irish branch of the Earl of Hopetoun's family and, sure, wasn't it a plague to have a good Scottish name and be cursed with an Irish brogue?

When he was not masquerading as Colonel Macdonald, he liked to escape to low taverns and thieves' kitchens, where he could be himself, and it was in one of these low dives that he first heard about the Waverley jewels. He was used to thieves' stories being either downright lies or wild exaggeration, and so he all but dismissed the story of the jewels from his mind.

That was until he met Lady Dexter in the street on the day of her musicale and heard about Miss Callow.

'I was never more surprised,' said Lady Dexter, 'for all the talk was that the girls were taken by Maria Waverley from an orphanage and had no relatives at all. In fact, she told me so herself. Then this Miss

Callow came to call. There is one Waverley girl left unmarried, Felicity, and this Miss Callow, who is the girl's aunt, wishes to bring her out. I had met Felicity Waverley, a glorious creature, so I told Miss Callow to bring her to my musicale this evening. But, I tell you, Colonel Macdonald, I was quite blinded by Miss Callow's jewels – if they are *her* jewels, for the Waverley jewels are famous, you know. Such fine stones! She must be quite a strong old lady, since the weight of all those gems must have been considerable.'

'I look forward to making her acquaintance,' said Colonel Macdonald.

'Don't let young Miss Waverley steal your heart away,' teased Lady Dexter, 'or we shall all be most terribly jealous.'

He kissed her hand. 'Now, who could tear me from your side?' he said in his soft, lazy brogue. 'You know I adore you.'

'Go on with you,' laughed Lady Dexter, but secretly she was delighted. She was nearly fifty, and Colonel Macdonald made her feel like a young girl.

The colonel sauntered on his way, his mind racing. This could be it. If he could charm this Waverley girl into marriage and get those jewels, he could flee the country and set himself up for life.

Felicity decided she could not stand the strain of arriving on her own and then lying about her 'aunt's' supposed indisposition, so she decided to gamble and see if she could make her explanations before she arrived. She accordingly sent a pathetic little note to

Lady Dexter, saying her aunt was ill and had begged her to go on her own but she feared to do so as it was a very shocking thing to do. A note from Lady Dexter was delivered back by one of her footmen. Miss Waverley must come alone. Her maid could escort her to the door, and Lady Dexter herself would introduce her to the company.

Colonel Macdonald's first feeling on beholding Felicity Waverley was one of dismay. He was used to hearing wealthy girls described as 'beautiful', meaning the girl's fortune lent her an allure. But Felicity Waverley *was* beautiful. When he first saw her, she was standing with Lady Dexter, being introduced to some people at the doorway of the music room. She was wearing a slip of a gown of white satin covered with an overdress of white French net decorated with a tiny blue spot. She had white silk roses in her hair, the center of each rose being formed of seed pearls and tiny sapphires. But she wore no other gems. Her white throat was bare and her gloved arms free of bracelets. He found himself daunted by her beauty and wishing she had worn some of the famous Waverley jewels to give him courage to woo her.

For the first time, his usual confidence deserted him. His previous victims had both been on the plain side. He squared his shoulders as if going into one of the battles he had so neatly avoided by deserting and bowed low before Lady Dexter. 'Introduce me to this enchantress, I command you!' he cried.

Lady Dexter looked amused and Miss Felicity Waverley decidedly annoyed. Lady Dexter performed the introductions and then, being hailed by a party of new arrivals, left Felicity with Colonel Macdonald.

'Your beauty leaves me dumbfounded,' said the gallant colonel. He heard his voice sounding in his own ears and realized with some irritation that his carefully cultivated Irish brogue was slipping into a decidedly Scottish burr.

'On the contrary, you appear to have plenty to say, sir,' said Felicity, fanning herself and looking over his shoulder. Bernard Anderson, his mother, and Lady Artemis were just entering the room. Lady Artemis said something to Bernard, who blushed. Felicity looked up at the colonel with new eyes. He was handsome and personable. Bernard must not see that she cared about his neglect one bit.

'You do not appreciate my compliments, I can see,' the colonel was saying.

'It is rather hard to know how to receive them,' said Felicity with a smile. 'I can either simper, hit you playfully with my fan, or walk away.'

'Then I had better try to be sensible,' he said. 'Oh, that my poor Irish tongue could find the magic to charm you.'

'Is that your way of trying to be sensible?' asked Felicity, beginning to be amused.

'Sure, it's the best I can do,' he said with a grin. 'Will you be after letting me fetch you a glass of something?'

'Delighted, sir. Ratafia will do.'

He bowed and left to find a glass of ratafia for her. His place was taken by the Marquess of Darkwater. 'Where is Miss Callow?' he asked. 'Not still indisposed.'

'Alas, yes, my lord.'

'You and your aunt are like those cunning little figures on a curiosity clock. You know, the clock chimes and little figures appear, one for rain and the other for sunshine, but never the two together.'

'We are both unfortunate in that we have suffered from bad health, but I am glad our misfortune provides you with amusement.'

'Your ill health does not amuse me, only the strange way it seems impossible to see the two of you together at the one time.'

Felicity affected a yawn and stared around the room as if seeking distraction. Bernard caught her eye and gave her a look like a whipped dog. His mother saw that look and stepped in front of him to block his view of Felicity.

'A word of warning in your ear, Miss Waverley,' Felicity heard the marquess say. 'Colonel Macdonald claims to be a Member of Parliament for Linlithgowshire, but there is no such place. I fear he is an impostor.'

'How interesting,' said Felicity languidly. 'Thank you for telling me, my lord. It adds a certain luster to his charm and looks, and adds spice to this dull evening. Ah, Colonel Macdonald. We were just talking about you.'

'Evening, Darkwater,' said the colonel cheerfully. The marquess ignored him completely, gave Felicity a stiff bow, and strode away.

'His spleen must be mortal bad,' declared the colonel.

'You are a Member of Parliament, I believe,' said Felicity.

'For my sins. Linlithgowshire – in Scotland.'

'I have heard of the town of Linlithgow in Lothian, but not of Linlithgowshire.'

'Oh, 'tis a small county,' said the colonel airily. 'The musicale is about to begin. May I have the honor of escorting you?'

Felicity's glance flicked over the guests, from the marquess's cold eyes to Bernard's sheepish ones, to Lady Artemis's mocking ones, and then she gave the colonel a radiant smile. 'With pleasure,' she said, placing her hand on his arm.

The musicale was unfortunately composed of amateur performers. Usually hostesses tried to secure the latest diva, but Lady Dexter considered such a practice a waste of money when there were so many ladies in society eager to perform for no fee whatsoever. Although she herself was a flirtatious and *mondaine* lady, she had a weakness for the company of middle-aged bluestockings, not the genuine ones, but the affected ones who considered that the way to compete with the masculine intellect was to roar out ballads in as deep a voice as possible.

Felicity felt the colonel pressing something into her hand. She looked down. Two little pieces of candle wax lay there. 'Earplugs,' whispered the colonel. Felicity gratefully popped the pieces of wax into her ears and endured the rest of the concert in an uncomfortable state of unease. It was not the muffled roar of the singers' voices nor yet the presence of the handsome colonel that was causing Felicity discomfort but an acute awareness that the Marquess of Darkwater was sitting behind her. She could sense his physical presence, and that presence seemed to be upsetting her body. She realized with a little shock that she was physically afraid of him, yet could not make sense of her feelings.

She could only be glad when the last red-faced lady had roared off into silence. She deftly removed the earplugs. 'Thank goodness that is over,' said the colonel cheerfully. 'Supper, I think, and let's hope the supper is good enough to make up for the ordeal we have just endured.'

The supper proved to be as good as he had hoped. He had a hard time enjoying the food, however, for Felicity kept asking him searching questions about the abolition of slavery and the Corn Laws, two subjects he knew little about and cared less.

He privately thought slavery was a great idea and the law that declared any black man setting foot anywhere in Britain was automatically a free citizen absolutely ridiculous. But it was fortunate he kept such views to himself. Felicity was now sure he was an impostor and adventurer and was amused by him, but she would never have forgiven him had she known he held such callous and unnatural views. Felicity regarded herself as an impostor, and that made her feel drawn to the colonel. She then asked him about his home in Ireland. The colonel, glad to be free from political questions, waxed eloquent over his family home. The fact that he had never been to Ireland and had never had a home since he had left the weaver's cottage he had been born in did not faze him. He described the old square building set among the gentle green hills of County Down and the fine stables he had and the splendid fishing on one of his own private lakes. He went on to describe the splendid alfresco meals he had had on the grounds of his estate when his cousin the Earl of Hopetoun and his family had come to stay. He conjured up mythical cousins and aunts and soon had Felicity in tears of laughter over their fictitious eccentricities. There was Aunt Jane who rode to hounds just like a man and swore like a trooper. There was gentle Aunt Phyllis who knitted garters for the peasantry, blind to the fact that the poor souls had no stockings to hold up. And there was roistering Uncle John, the terror of the neighborhood when he was in his cups. He told story after story, and Felicity listened to him, wide-eyed, delighted with his handsome face, soft voice, and his hilarious stories about the members of his family. By the end of supper, she was beginning to believe there might even be a place called Linlithgowshire.

The colonel had found out she had come unescorted and quickly secured permission from Lady Dexter to escort Miss Waverley home by riding alongside her carriage.

He promised to take her driving on the following day. Felicity smiled as she undressed for bed that night. Bernard was forgotten. She did not care if the colonel was an impostor. He was kind and funny and he made her laugh. And then, all at once, the smile died on her lips. She could feel the presence of the Marquess of

Darkwater so strongly that she looked wildly about the room. With a little shiver, she climbed into bed, feeling haunted.

At that very same moment, the Marquess of Darkwater finished a letter to the Earl of Hopetoun telling that peer there was a certain Colonel Macdonald in London who was not only claiming to be M.P. for Linlithgowshire but to be a cousin of the earl. He sanded the letter and decided to send his servant off with it in the morning to catch the royal mail to Edinburgh. The new fast coaches only took thirty-four-and-a-half hours to reach the capital of Scotland. He had paid for a return reply. With any luck, he should hear from Hopetoun before another week was out. Damn Felicity Waverley. He should leave her to her fate. But somehow, he just could not get that girl out of his mind . . .

Felicity decided to spend the earlier part of the following afternoon as Miss Callow and then change back to herself to go driving with the colonel.

Her first caller, to her surprise, was Bernard Anderson. When he learned Felicity was 'out', he looked ready to flee rather than spend any time with Miss Callow, but Felicity in her role as her own aunt pressed him to stay for tea.

'You look very disturbed, young man,' she croaked. 'What is amiss?'

'I had hoped to see Miss Felicity,' said Bernard wretchedly. 'You see . . .'

He broke off and got to his feet in blushing confusion as the famous actress Caroline James was announced.

Caroline's blue eyes twinkled as she surveyed Felicity in the guise of Miss Callow.

'I am delighted to see you,' said Felicity. 'Felicity is out at the moment. She will be devastated to have missed you. May I present Mr Bernard Anderson to you? Mr Anderson, Miss Caroline James.'

'I say,' said Bernard, thanking his stars his mother was not present. 'I have seen you many times on the stage, Miss James. Such divine acting! Your Lady Macbeth quite frightened me.'

'Thank you,' said Caroline. 'I mean, I should have hated to have played a Lady Macbeth people actually liked. Do you attend the playhouse often, Mr Anderson?'

'When I can,' said Bernard eagerly. He meant when he could escape from his matchmaking mama.

'I am sorry not to see Felicity,' said Caroline. 'It may surprise you to learn, Mr Anderson, that Miss Waverley was the one who gave me the courage to go back on the stage instead of entering into a marriage that would, I am now convinced, have made me miserable. Of course, this all may seem strange to a young bachelor like yourself. Men do not know what it is like to be constrained to marry someone out of fear of insecurity or because a pushing parent demands the sacrifice.'

'Oh, yes, they do,' said Bernard in a hollow voice, and Caroline looked at him curiously.

Tea was brought in by Mrs Ricketts. Felicity sank back into the shadow of her wing chair and watched with amusement as Bernard began to relax and talk easily in Caroline's company. Caroline was looking particularly fine in a blue velvet carriage dress with a wide-brimmed black velvet hat on her head. Felicity found she was glad she had not had to meet Bernard as herself. It had been a stupid idea even to think of marrying him. He was too puppyish, too naive, and too much under the thumb of his mother. The colonel on the other hand was tall and mature and very amusing. One would never be bored. She roused herself with a glance at the clock and realized she would need to get rid of her guests, for it would take her a full hour to take off her disguise.

Bernard and Caroline left together. 'I do not have my carriage, ma'am,' said Bernard eagerly, 'but I would be honored to escort you.'

'Very well,' said Caroline, and Bernard waved down a passing hack.

When they reached Caroline's address in Covent Garden, Bernard helped her down, paid the hack, and stood on the pavement with a sort of extinguished look on his face that went straight to Caroline's heart.

'Something is troubling you,' she said gently. 'I do not have to be at the theater for two hours yet. Come upstairs and we can sit and chat.'

Her flat was a modest apartment above a bakery. It was all exotic and exciting to Bernard – the cozy parlor with a screen in the corner plastered with playbills, various theatrical costumes and plays lying about, the cheerful fire, the noises of the street coming up from outside and the general feeling of freedom.

He drank wine and looked dreamily at the fire

while Caroline went into her bedroom and changed into a loose-flowing gown and then came back and sat on the other side of the fire and said, 'Now tell me all about it.'

And Bernard did. All about his mother, all about how he was being forced into marriage with Lady Artemis – 'and she frightens me,' he said. 'She is such a *knowing* sort of lady.'

'Did you hope to court Felicity?' asked Caroline.

'I don't know now,' said Bernard. 'I thought it would be jolly to have a friend my own age, but Mama . . . Well, there you are. She holds the purse strings.'

'What would you do if . . . I mean, say you were free to work for your living; what would you do?'

Bernard ran his hands through his thick fair hair and stared at her wildly. 'What would I do? Oh, ma'am, I would be a carpenter.'

'A worthy trade. You would need to serve an apprenticeship.'

'But I have,' exclaimed Bernard. 'When my father was alive, we lived in Mealchin in Berkshire. There was a carpenter in the village and he taught me all his skills. My father – he died two years ago – was amused by my enthusiasm, but my mother was furious. She could not do anything to stop me when father was alive, but when he died, well, it transpired she had set her heart on me marrying an heiress and so we moved to town. I am a simple sort of chap, really, and would have made an excellent tradesman. Life is very unfair. There is probably some poor carpenter somewhere who dreams of how wonderful life would be if he could only be a gentleman of leisure and go to all the ton parties.'

'No doubt. I am afraid you must excuse me now, Mr Anderson. I am due at the playhouse.'

Bernard thought of his mother's disapproving face; he thought of Lady Artemis, who made him feel so awkward and clumsy and gauche. He clasped his hands together and stared at Caroline James. 'Oh, how I would love to watch you from the wings,' he said. 'To be a part of the theater. To be behind the scenes.'

'That can most certainly be arranged,' said Caroline. 'But your mother will be waiting for you.'

'Let her wait,' said Bernard. 'Please . . .'

'How old are you?'

'Twenty.'

'A great age,' said Caroline with a mocking smile.

'I am a *man*,' declared Bernard, standing up and striking his breast in the best Haymarket manner.

'And I am turned thirty,' said Caroline, 'an old lady compared to your youth. Oh, very well. You may come with me. But do not get in anyone's way!'

The play in which Caroline was appearing was called *The Beau's Delight or Miss Polly's Fancy*, a light-weight piece of nonsense that was drawing large crowds. At several points in her performance, she remembered Bernard and glanced toward the wings, both right and left, but of her young cavalier, there was no sign. It was the last night of the play, and the theater was crowded to the gods. When it was over, she sat in her dressing room removing her makeup. The manager of the playhouse entered. 'I want to talk to you about that young fellow you brought along,' he said.

'I'm sorry,' said Caroline quickly. 'He is in love with the theater. I thought it would do no harm. I assume he made a nuisance of himself and you sent him packing.'

'On the contrary,' said the manager, Mr Josiah Biggs, drawing up a chair and sitting down by the small coal fire, 'he has made himself very useful. That is what I want to talk to you about. He repaired some scenery for me in a trice. So deft and busy with his fingers! I fell into conversation with him. We began to talk about transformation scenes, and he got some paper and a pencil and drew out plans for a stupendous waterfall operated by a clockwork device, not like that tin thing at Vauxhall, but using real water.'

'You would flood the stage and drown the harlequin,' said Caroline.

'Not the way your Mr Anderson has planned it. Is he really a gentleman?'

'I am afraid so, and one with a mother who would tear you limb from limb.'

'I could be the talk of the nation with such a device as that waterfall,' said the manager dreamily. 'You gave up marriage to a baron to stay on the stage. Why should not this Mr Anderson amuse himself by working with us for a little?'

'Colonel Bridie was not a baron when I knew him,' said Caroline, 'although I would have given him up just the same. But this is different. I was an actress in my youth and returned to the theater. It would not answer.'

'I have given him the offer of a job.'

'He cannot take it. He goes in fear of his mother.'

But Bernard, who joined the party in the Green Room that night, appeared to have forgotten his mother's very existence. His eyes were shining, there was sawdust on his coat, and he was talking happily to various members of the cast. When Caroline took her leave, she found Bernard at her elbow.

'I am going to escort you home,' said Bernard firmly. He appeared to have grown in stature in one evening.

When Caroline reached the baker's shop under her flat, she turned to Bernard and held out her hand. 'Good night, Mr Anderson,' she said firmly.

Bernard held tightly onto her hand. 'I was offered a job this evening,' he said proudly.

'So I heard,' said Caroline, trying to tug her hand free.

'Might I not come up with you and talk about it for a little?'

Caroline's face hardened. 'Certainly not!'

'Oh, just for a little, please, Miss James. This has been the most wonderful evening of my life.'

Caroline relaxed. Mr Anderson really just wanted to talk.

'Just for a little,' she said, 'and then you really must be on your way.'

Mrs Anderson paced up and down the hall of her town house all night long, listening to the hoarse call of the watch, waiting for her son to come home. She had had to attend a rout on her own. Lady Artemis Verity had been there, and because of Bernard's absence, Lady Artemis had spent most of her time talking to that ex-fiancé of hers, Mr Fordyce. Pale dawn light began to creep into the hall. Mrs Anderson began to feel seriously alarmed. Bernard must have been attacked by footpads.

And then at six o'clock she heard his key in the lock. Bernard came in quietly. 'Morning, Mother,' he said coolly, and made for the stairs.

Mrs Anderson's massive bosom swelled. 'Have you nothing to say to me?' she cried, head back, eyes flashing fire.

'No, Mother,' said Bernard quietly. 'Nothing at all.'

Speechless with amazement, she watched him mount the stairs to his room.

FOUR

While Bernard Anderson fell into a dreamless sleep, Felicity awoke. She drew back the bed hangings and looked at the little French gilt clock on the mantelpiece. She turned over on her side and tried to go back to sleep, but her mind was racing.

Fragments of conversation with Colonel Macdonald floated through her head. 'I have never been married. I never before found anyone I was willing to share my life with . . . until now.'

It was as good as a proposal of marriage. She had spent last evening in a mood of happy elation. But what now of all her previous strictures and beliefs about that prison called marriage? She had always considered marriage a sort of genteel serfdom. But life with the colonel would never be dull. He was so happy and carefree. He had admitted with an endearingly rueful smile that he had little money. Felicity had confessed that although she did not have a bank balance, she did have the Waverley jewels and was about to start selling a few in order to pay the servants and to cover the daily expenses of running the house. Colonel Macdonald had promptly said if she would trust him with them, he could get her a very good price, so Felicity had agreed to hand a few items to him that very afternoon.

The Marquess of Darkwater's handsome, saturnine face rose in her mind's eye again, and his caution rang in her ears. Had she been too trusting? Everyone knew about the Marquess of Darkwater, his unlucky marriage and his background. No one seemed to know much about the colonel apart from what he told them. Lady Dexter had sung the colonel's praises, but when Felicity had pointed out the colonel was a very odd sort of politician in that he seemed to fight shy of political subjects, Lady Dexter had laughed and said he never bored the ladies with tedious discussions. Felicity was lonely. She realized that was the root of her problem.

Felicity frowned. She should really write to either Frederica or Fanny, begging their forgiveness and so put an end to loneliness. But she was an independent lady, a published author. She should not be so weak-kneed.

But as the time for the colonel's call approached, Felicity, sorting out a few jewels, became more and more worried about Colonel Macdonald. It certainly would not hurt to lose such a few trinkets when she had so many, yet, because she was a woman and alone, pride made her want to be sure she was not being gulled.

As a young miss, she could hardly interrogate the colonel. But in the guise of her aunt, Miss Callow, she could ask as many searching questions as she wanted.

With great care, she donned her disguise and then went down to the drawing room and waited for the colonel to arrive. On a small table beside her, she placed two fine rings, one ruby and one sapphire, and a collar of diamonds. Mrs Ricketts was ordered to draw the curtains but to light only one candle and to place it on the table next to the jewels. Felicity wanted to keep the colonel's attention on the flashing jewels and not on herself.

The colonel was ushered in. At first he looked taken aback to find 'Miss Callow' and not Felicity, but then his eye fell on the jewels and he found he could not look away.

He was sorely in need of money. Triumphant and sure of Felicity, he had gambled heavily the night before and had lost a large sum of money to a Mr Herd, a wealthy landowner. But the colonel had already lost money on a previous occasion to this same Mr Herd, and Mr Herd coldly said he expected to be paid promptly. The colonel had promised to meet him after he had seen Felicity. He would use the money for the jewels to pay Mr Herd, tell Felicity the jeweler would pay a sum the following week, and then in the intervening week, do his damnedest to get her to promise to marry him.

'My appointment was with Miss Felicity,' he said to the little old lady in the high wing chair.

'I know,' said Felicity, 'and I know why you are come.'

The colonel wrenched his eyes away from the jewels and looked at her directly and then quickly averted his gaze. Gad! What an ugly birthmark. Had Felicity changed her mind?

'Sit down,' commanded Miss Callow. 'I believe you have offered to sell a few items of jewelry for us.'

Colonel Macdonald heaved a sigh of relief. The game was still on.

'Yes, ma'am,' he said. 'I would do anything to be of service to Miss Felicity.' He was about to boldly add he had also come to ask leave to pay his respects, but then no doubt Miss Callow would proceed to ask him all about his income and prospects. Better persuade Felicity herself.

Felicity shrank back further into the shadows in order to study him better. She could see he was nervous and uneasy, but it did not seem the uneasiness of the lover.

She leaned slightly forward. 'Felicity tells me you are a Member of Parliament.'

'Yes, ma'am.'

'There is a bill at present being read in the House that interests me. It is—'

'Ah, sure,' he interrupted quickly, 'you must not be bothering your poor head with such things, ma'am. You see, I can get a good deal for those jewels if I get them to the man quickly.' He half rose.

'Please remain seated,' said Felicity. She felt a wave of sadness engulf her. The colonel was not interested in turning his charm on what he thought was an ugly old woman, and his eyes, which were fastened on the jewels, held a naked look of avarice. Thank goodness I have discovered what he is really like in time, thought Felicity. Aloud she said, 'I do not see any need for haste, Mr Macdonald. Nor do I now wish the Waverley jewels to go to some anonymous jeweler. I shall take them myself to Rundell & Bridge. So much safer to deal with a known and reputable firm.'

The colonel felt a sharp stab of fear somewhere in the pit of his stomach. He had put it about society that he was in easy circumstances. If he did not pay his gambling debts, then he would need to flee London. He had become accustomed to luxuries. His credit with his tailor, his club, his grocers, and his wine merchants had run out. He did not want to start off again penniless in some provincial city. He looked at the jewels again. He could raise enough on those to take him to Paris, and there he could emerge with a new identity and play the field. It was a pity about Felicity, for it would have been grand to have had the pleasure of such a beauty in his bed.

Still, he tried. 'Come now, ma'am,' he cajoled. 'Let me be speaking with Miss Felicity herself, and she will vouch for my good character.'

'Miss Felicity is guided by me in all matters,' said Felicity. 'I wish to retire.' She reached out a hand for the bell.

'Don't touch that, or it will be the worse for ye!'

Felicity looked up in amazement. Colonel

Macdonald had got to his feet and was drawing a wicked-looking knife from his pocket.

And then downstairs came a knocking at the street door. 'Stay still,' hissed the colonel, holding the point of the knife at her throat. 'Not a word.'

From downstairs came the Marquess of Darkwater's voice and Mrs Ricketts's answering one saying that Miss Felicity was out and that Miss Callow was entertaining someone and perhaps would not like to be disturbed but she would go and find out.

The colonel backed away until he was standing behind the door. 'If you value your life, you old baggage,' he hissed, 'you will tell her to send Darkwater away.'

Felicity stared at him in baffled fury. But if she did not obey, then he might stab Mrs Ricketts as well.

'Do not come in,' said Felicity as Mrs Ricketts appeared in the doorway. 'Tell the marquess I am not free.'

'Yes, mum,' said Mrs Ricketts. She turned and went away.

'Good,' whispered the colonel. 'We will sit and wait until the coast is clear, and then we will go to your bedchamber, old lady, and we will find the rest of the jewels.'

'You will hang, you greedy scoundrel,' said Felicity.

Colonel Macdonald shrugged. 'May as well be hanged for a sheep as a lamb.'

Downstairs, Mrs Ricketts held open the street door for the marquess. 'Miss Callow does not wish to be disturbed,' she said in a loud voice. But as the marquess made to leave, she caught his arm and whispered urgently, 'Please go up, sir. Something is wrong. I know it.' She slammed the door loudly so that anyone listening would think the marquess had left.

The marquess looked at her in surprise and then ran lightly up the stairs.

He stopped short at the tableau that met his eyes. Miss Callow was shrinking back in her chair while the colonel held a long sharp knife in front of her.

The colonel saw him. 'Come one step nearer, and I will kill her,' he said.

Unnoticed by him, Felicity had been slowly drawing up her knees. As the marquess hesitated, Felicity kicked out with all her might, the serviceable half boots she considered correct dress for an old lady striking the colonel full in the stomach. As he doubled up, the marquess moved like lightning and struck him full on the chin with a massive blow of his fist. The colonel was driven backward by the blow. He crashed into a chair opposite, then crumpled up and lay half across it, dead to the world.

'Oh, bravo!' cried Felicity, leaping to her feet, 'A flush hit, sir. Bravo!'

The marquess took off his gloves, took out his handkerchief, and wound it around his bleeding knuckles. Then he looked at Miss Callow, and a flash of amusement lit up his eyes. Her white wig had slipped to one side revealing the glossy chestnut hair of Felicity Waverley.

'I mean,' quavered Felicity, remembering her role all too late, 'we are monstrous pleased to be rescued.'

The servants came running in, Mrs Ricketts carrying a length of cord with which she proceeded to tie up the colonel.

'Drag him out to the landing and shut the door,' ordered the marquess, 'and give me a few minutes in private with Miss Callow.'

'Yes, my lord,' said Mrs Ricketts. 'Mary, Beth, Joan, seize a hold of this fellow.'

They removed the colonel by pulling his unconscious body to the floor and then sliding it across the rugs and out onto the landing. Mrs Ricketts turned in the doorway. She tried to signal to Felicity that her wig was askew, but Felicity was looking at the marquess. But the marquess saw Mrs Ricketts and jerked his head. She gave a resigned sort of curtsy and withdrew, closing the door behind her.

'The jig is up, Miss Felicity,' said the marquess.

'Yes, I am so glad that villain has been unmasked,' said Felicity. She sat down in the wing chair. One of the wings caught at her wig and it and the cap she was wearing fell off and landed on the floor.

The marquess began to laugh. 'I mean *you* have been unmasked, Miss Felicity. What a fright you have made of yourself!'

Tears started to Felicity's eyes. 'So you know,' she said weakly.

The amusement left his face. 'Come, Miss Felicity. Go abovestairs and change back to your normal and beautiful appearance while I deal with the authorities.'

Felicity nodded dumbly, too upset to protest. But she scooped up the jewels before she left the room. She was so rattled by the colonel's attack on her, she was worried the marquess might prove to be a thief as well.

The marquess went out after her, stepped over the colonel's unconscious body, and told Mrs Ricketts, who was waiting in the hall, that he would return shortly with the constable and a magistrate.

Upstairs, Felicity wearily removed her disguise. She felt terribly lost and tired. All around her in the west end of London were young misses with mothers and fathers to turn to in an emergency. Her thoughts turned again to the mother she had never known, and she longed to give up completely, to lie facedown on the bed and cry her eyes out.

Colonel Macdonald recovered consciousness. He cautiously felt with his fingers at his bound wrists. Feverishly he began to work at the knots. The rope was thick, and Mrs Ricketts had not made a very good job of tying him up. Soon he had his wrists free and then his ankles. For one mad moment, he thought of trying to get at least some of those jewels. But Darkwater might be somewhere about, and if he were not, he would surely be returning with the forces of law and order. Groggily the colonel got to his feet. He slid down the banisters. Mrs Ricketts had left her post in the hall to go down to the kitchens. He quietly opened the door and walked down the stairs and then he began to run as hard as he could, down toward the river, down to where that sordid network of alleys, wharves, and slums would swallow him up.

The marquess was furious when he returned to find the colonel had escaped. But he sat with Felicity while the magistrate, the beadle, and the constable asked questions. When they had finally taken their leave, he said quietly to Felicity, 'I did not tell the authorities of your ridiculous masquerade. Now tell me why you found it necessary to pretend to be your own aunt. Were you trying to chaperone *yourself* at the Season?'

Felicity nodded dumbly.

The marquess looked at her bent head. 'Have you no one to care of you, my child?'

'No, my lord. Except, of course, Mrs Ricketts.'

'A housekeeper, however worthy, is not enough to protect you from charlatans. Colonel Macdonald pretended he was going to sell some jewels for you. Why? Are you so destitute?'

'No, my lord. I own this house and all the Waverley jewels. I have no money in the bank and wanted to sell a few items.'

He glanced about him. The money she had received for her book would certainly only last a short time in Regency London. He had an impulse to tell her he knew she was the author of *The Love Match*, but decided against it.

'Then I suggest,' he said, 'that you allow me to escort you to a reputable jeweler, where you may sell the items yourself. Tell me what you know of your family. The other two Waverley girls, Fanny and Frederica, are now titled ladies. Can you not write to them and ask them for protection?'

Felicity hung her head. 'I cannot. I quarreled with them. I do not know if they have forgiven me.'

He rang the bell and ordered tea to be brought

in; Quite like the master of the house, thought Mrs Ricketts with dawning hope.

He waited in silence while tea was served and while the obviously upset Felicity had time to compose herself.

'Begin at the beginning,' he said, 'and tell me how you came to be in this odd situation.'

Felicity spread her hands in a gesture of resignation. Then she began to speak.

'We were taken from an orphanage, that is, I and Fanny and Frederica, by Mrs Waverley and brought up in an odd way. We were allowed little social life; we were constantly warned against the evils of men and marriage. Mrs Waverley is a very good teacher, and she educated us herself. Then Fanny ran away to get married, and later Frederica. But Mrs Waverley herself deserted me to get married to Colonel Bridie, now Baron Meldon. She left me this house, as I told you, and all those wretched jewels. There is a considerable amount of fine jewelry. Mrs Waverley would make us dress very drably when we went out but liked to attire us as richly as barbaric princesses when she entertained at home. I felt Fanny had betrayed me, and then I tried to prevent Frederica's marriage, for I really truly believed Lord Harry Danger did not mean to marry her. Both the Earl of Tredair, who married Fanny, and Lord Harry made attempts to find out the mystery of our parentage but were both unsuccessful. Since Mrs Waverley had almost convinced us we were all foundlings and bastards, we might have let the matter rest. But it did seem as if someone or some people were determined to stop us from finding out anything.' She gave an embarrassed laugh. 'We even began to think we might be royal bastards, for every time Mrs Waverley saw the Prince Regent, she turned white and he looked monstrous upset. Then the orphanage itself only housed girls who were being kept there by wealthy relatives. They told us we were charity cases, but I found that hard to believe as no one on the ruling body of that orphanage showed any signs of charity whatsoever.

'I decided never to marry. I agreed with Mrs Waverley's views, even though she had betrayed them, because women are the lesser sex and marriage is a form of slavery. But I began to think there might possibly be exceptions to the rule,' said Felicity wistfully. 'I hear reports that both Fanny and Frederica are very happy. I was . . . I am . . . lonely. I thought, don't you see, that being of independent means I could perhaps find a companion, an equal. Yes, I suspected Colonel Macdonald was an impostor, but he seemed so gay, so charming, and I am by way of being an impostor myself. Baron Meldon, who married Mrs Waverley, was at one time engaged to the actress Caroline James. She called here, and I hit on the plan of being made up to look like an elderly lady. That way I could chaperone myself. Now you have discovered my trick; there is nothing left for me but to settle down to a solitary existence.'

'But what is stopping you from writing to Lady Tredair or Lady Harry?' asked the marquess.

Felicity sighed. 'We were brought up to be rivals.

Pride, combined with fear they might still be angry with me – that is what is stopping me.'

She fell silent. He sat opposite her, very much at his ease, the candlelight shining on his handsome face. He studied her for some moments, noticing the purity of her skin and the gleaming cascade of her chestnut hair.

'I sometimes hate Mrs Waverley,' said Felicity suddenly.

'And yet,' he said, 'she saved you from the orphanage and left you independent. She educated you well and made you all so independent-minded that at least Fanny and Frederica found two gentlemen who were prepared to treat them as equals, or so I believe.'

'Perhaps,' said Felicity slowly. 'But I think I hate her because I feel in my bones she knows the identity of our parents. Before she met the baron, she was very possessive and did everything to bind us close to her, almost as if she had bought herself a ready-made family to protect her from the world.'

There was another long silence, and he shifted restlessly, and she wondered whether he was becoming bored, and that thought gave her a sharp pain. Soon he would rise to take his leave, his curiosity satisfied, and she would never see him again.

'It is a fascinating mystery,' he said. 'Have courage, Miss Felicity. Surely you and I would be better employed finding out where you come from than spending our evenings in hot rooms talking to a lot of charlatans and bores.'

'I do not see how we can succeed where Tredair and Danger failed,' said Felicity.

'They were both men deeply in love, and having secured their hearts' desire, they lost interest,' said the marquess. 'But we, Miss Felicity, are heart-free and intelligent. Before we set about our investigations, we must find a chaperone for you. No, do not look so surprised. I know what you are thinking. I shall not tell anyone of your masquerade. As far as society is concerned, Miss Callow has retired to the country. Now, I have a fourth cousin, resident in London, a poor relation. I had planned to do something about her plight, for she is companion to an old harridan and having quite a miserable time of it. Allow me to fetch her here. We may have to travel, and you cannot drive off with me on your own.'

From being in the depths of misery, Felicity began to feel quite light-headed with excitement. She clasped her hands together and looked at him beseechingly. 'It would be wonderful if we could solve the mystery.'

He raised an admonitory finger. 'Be warned, Miss Felicity, that the outcome may not be what you hope.'

'Anything is better than not knowing,' said Felicity. 'Where do we start?'

'I think,' he said, 'we will start with Mrs Waverley herself.'

The marquess's fourth cousin, Miss Agnes Joust, was a thoroughly silly woman, and was suffering as much as any woman without any strength of character can when she finds herself in a nasty predicament. Miss Joust had survived three months as companion to a Mrs Deves-Pereneux. Mrs Deves-Pereneux was a gross, overfed bully. Miss Joust was thin and faded and fortyish. The only thing that lightened her days was the knowledge that her handsome relative, the Marquess of Darkwater, was in London. She had not seen him for many years until he had called on her a bare month ago. Miss Joust had fallen violently in love with him on the spot. She wrote him little notes about the happenings of her days. Occasionally he would reply, and she kept his letters in a sandalwood box on her toilet table, reading and rereading them. One of her favorite dreams was that he would arrive in person again, but this time he would sweep her off, away from the horrible Mrs Deves-Pereneux.

Miss Joust had no faith to console her. Every Sunday for the past three months she had prayed for deliverance from her mistress, and every Monday came along to show that God had not paid any attention. Therefore, it followed that God did not exist, and Miss Joust became determined to punish Him by telling Him so. Mrs Deves-Pereneux liked to walk home from church. It was half a mile, and the going was slow and painful for both women – for Mrs Deves-Pereneux because she was fat and for Miss Joust because her mistress leaned too heavily on her arm and grumbled and wheezed.

They were just reaching the bleak red brick house in Bloomsbury where Mrs Deves-Pereneux lived when Miss Joust saw a smart curricle approaching and her heart began to hammer hard as she recognized the driver.

'Why, 'tis Lord Darkwater,' she cried.

'What's he want?' grumbled Mrs Deves-Pereneux.

'Got no right to come calling on servants without a by-your-leave, and so I shall tell him.'

Tears started to Miss Joust's weak eyes. Mrs Deves-Pereneux, a frightful old snob, had no intention of being rude to a lord, but it did her heart good to torment Miss Joust.

But the old lady was quite put out when the marquess said he wished to see Miss Joust in private. 'Servants,' said Mrs Deves-Pereneux nastily, 'have to give notice when they are expecting callers.'

'I was under the understanding that Miss Joust was your companion,' said the marquess icily as he followed them into the gloom of the downstairs parlor.

'Well, well, *paid* companion,' said the old lady, but in a mollified tone, for she had noticed Miss Joust's nose had turned red, a sure sign of acute distress. 'I shall retire for a few moments, my lord, and then you may have the honor of taking tea with me.'

'That will not be possible,' he said coldly. 'My time is short.'

Miss Joust groaned inwardly. A few moments bliss in his company would mean days of cruelty as Mrs Deves-Pereneux exacted her revenge. An hour, say, would have made such treatment bearable.

As soon as her mistress had lumbered out, Miss Joust began on a long, prepared speech, well-rehearsed for just such an occasion. But he interrupted her and said, 'I had hoped to do things pleasantly, but that old fright never does anything pleasant. I have found a congenial post for you, Miss Joust. Go and get your trunk packed. We will leave immediately.'

Miss Joust clasped her hands to her bosom. The marquess's well-tailored coat of Bath superfine and leather breeches and top boots faded to be replaced by a suit of shining armor. Somewhere in her ears she could hear a celestial choir and the snort of his milk-white steed outside the door.

'Are you all right, Miss Joust?' asked the marquess anxiously, for her eyes were now closed and she was breathing rapidly.

Miss Joust opened her eyes. 'I will do as you command, my lord,' she said firmly, 'and escape this dungeon!'

With head thrown back, she strode out of the room.

The marquess experienced a qualm of doubt and then reassured himself with the thought that half the spinster companions and chaperones in London were decidedly weird.

Then there came sounds of the very devil of a row, coming from upstairs. He could hear the deep bass of Mrs Deves-Pereneux's voice punctuated with the shrill protests of Miss Joust.

The afternoon dragged on, the noise upstairs went on and on, the clocks ticked, and the fire died in the hearth. The marquess was just about to rouse himself and go upstairs to find out what was going on when the door opened and a much-flushed and exhilarated Miss Joust stood there, carrying a trunk, while the bulk of her mistress loomed behind her.

Mrs Deves-Pereneux's curses and complaints followed them from the house. The marquess could not be bothered telling her what he thought of her and so pretended to have been struck deaf.

'You will be relieved never to see her again,' he remarked as he drove through the streets of Bloomsbury.

'Oh, my lord, you have saved me from the jaws of hell,' exclaimed Miss Joust, and then in a more practical tone, 'Where are we going?'

'There is a young lady in need of a companion.'

'Young? How young?'

'Nineteen or twenty, I should guess.'

'Oh.'

'I had better tell you the whole story.'

As the marquess talked, Miss Joust began to feel more at ease. This Felicity had had a weird upbringing. And a bluestocking! Bluestockings were notoriously ugly. Nothing more tedious for a man than the company of a young bluestocking. Mature men like the marquess must find the feminine company of a *mondaine* older woman like herself infinitely preferable. For Miss Joust lived in a fantasy world. When she looked in her glass, she did not see a long-nosed spinster with drab brown hair and thin lips, but a calm, medieval beauty with an air of mystery. She was still convinced the vicar of the church in which she had prayed so uselessly to God was in love with her and had not declared his passion because of the fearsome Mrs Deves-Pereneux. The fact that the marquess might have arrived because of some divine intervention did not occur to Miss Joust. She had shown Him she could manage very well on her own, thank you, and so she did not believe in Him.

Felicity and Miss Joust sized each other up like two

stray cats. Felicity decided quickly that Miss Joust would do. She appeared to be a silly, nervous woman, but not a bully. Miss Joust was taken aback initially by Felicity's beauty, but she quickly recovered. It was just like the gallant marquess to offer to help Miss Waverley, but he would soon discover she came from very low origins indeed. One had only to look at her! No lady was ever so obviously beautiful. One had only to look at Emma Hamilton. Low origins meant Miss Waverley would remain unmarriageable. Miss Joust had not yet learned the happy fate of the other two Waverley girls.

There was, moreover, nothing of the lover in the marquess's demeanor. Miss Joust, her main worry laid to rest, was able to appreciate her comfortable surroundings, the finely appointed bedchamber allotted to her, and the excellence of the cuisine. Her head was full of dreams. They were to set out for Meldon in two days' time to confront Mrs Waverley. Miss Joust could see it now: Mrs Waverley would produce papers proving Felicity's father had been a low felon. The marquess would fall very silent and then he would seek her out. 'You cannot stay in such a household,' he would say. Miss Joust, wearing her best lilac sarcenet with her hair loose, would exclaim, 'Alas, what is to become of me?' He would then gaze at her with a smoldering look and reply, 'Fear not. I have found you another position.' 'Where?' demanded Miss Joust. 'What as?' 'As my wife,' he cried, seizing her in his arms. And that was such a lovely dream that Miss Joust smiled dreamily all through dinner and paid little attention to Felicity, who wondered whether to be cross or amused.

Miss Joust decided to pay attention to her surroundings by the time the pudding was brought in. That way, she could save a little of the splendid dream for bedtime. 'How do you pass your days in London, Miss Waverley?' she asked.

'Really, Miss Joust, I have just been telling you how I pass my days. Are you usually so inattentive?'

'Oh, no, Miss Waverley. I am just so glad to be away from that dreadful woman. So fatiguing. She quite addled my poor wits. Do tell me again.'

'Firstly, you may call me Felicity, and I shall call you Agnes. I do not have much in the way of a social life. I read a great deal. Do you read much, Agnes?'

'Yes, though I have not had the leisure to indulge my tastes of late. Mrs Deves-Pereneux would have me read to her quite shocking and unsuitable books, you know. *The Love Match* was the last book. Quite dreadful. As if any woman of society would be so loose in her morals.'

'I thought it was an excellent book,' said Felicity crossly. 'Why should people read books about rakes and philanderers with complacency yet shudder at the idea of a woman doing the same thing?'

'Ah, you are young, Felicity. Ladies have a natural modesty that curbs their actions. We all know we are put on this earth to be the support of some gentleman, as the ivy wraps itself around the strong oak.'

'Well put,' said Felicity acidly. 'Ivy is a parasite and will soon destroy the strong oak with its clinging dependency.'

'La! How fierce you are. Simon told me you were a bluestocking.'

'Simon?'

'The Marquess of Darkwater.'

'Forgive my ignorance, Agnes. I am not on such terms of familiarity with his lordship as to call him by his Christian name, or even to know of it.'

'It is different in my case,' said Agnes Joust, her nose turning pink. Her nose turned red when angry and pink when she was lying. 'Us being related, you know.'

'With relatives as rich as Darkwater in your family, I am surprised you have to earn your living,' commented Felicity.

'Well, one does not want to be a burden and . . .' Agnes was about to add that she was just one of many indigent relatives but thought better of it. 'Would you like me to read to you, Felicity?'

'No, thank you. I am perfectly capable of reading to myself.'

'Perhaps you would like me to demonstrate an interesting new stitch?'

'Do not be so worried about earning your keep,' said Felicity with quick sympathy. 'Your main job will be to chaperone me on our travels. In the meantime, you may rest as much as you like.'

Agnes felt a sudden rush of gratitude for Felicity. Such a pity she wasn't a lady.

Felicity was glad to retire to the privacy of her room as soon as possible. She looked wearily at the few pages of manuscript on her desk. Would she ever write another book?

FIVE

The next day, Felicity checked over the inventory of the Waverley jewels, the huge box that now held them open on her bedroom floor. She was wondering where she could put them for safekeeping. She had removed the items she meant to sell that day. As she was kneeling on the floor, bending over the box, there came a faint scratching on the door and Agnes walked in. She stopped short at the sight of the jewels, blazing like a pirate's treasure.

'I do not like to be disturbed before noon,' said Felicity shortly.

'Oh, what wondrous gems!' cried Agnes. She walked slowly forward, her eyes shining. 'Oh, how I would love to be able to wear jewels like that!'

'I am wondering where to put them for safekeeping,' said Felicity, half-irritated, half-amused by her companion's raptures. 'You may choose something to wear today, if it would please you.'

Agnes fell to her knees beside Felicity and began to lift piece after piece out of the box, holding the jewels up to the light. 'Do not take all day,' snapped Felicity. 'Select something and be off with you.'

Agnes seized an emerald necklace and bracelet from one of the many trays and darted from the room.

'It is not at all the thing, you know,' said Felicity later when Agnes joined her in the drawing room, 'to wear such gaudy baubles with a morning gown.'

'Oh, I know,' breathed Agnes, 'but just for this little while. I feel like a queen.'

'Mr Bernard Anderson has called,' said the house-keeper from the door of the drawing room.

Felicity hesitated and then said, 'Send him up, Ricketts.'

Bernard entered at a half run. He fell to his knees in front of the startled Felicity and cried, 'Oh, I am in love, and I am so very happy!'

Agnes let out a squawk and darted from the room and shut the door. She went halfway down the stairs, her hand to her breast, her heart beating hard. How wonderful. That very personable young man was obviously proposing to Felicity, and Felicity would accept him, and she, Agnes Joust, would be maid of honor, and the marquess would squeeze her hand tenderly and whisper in her ear, 'This wedding has given me the idea of marriage, Miss Joust . . . or may I call you . . . beloved?'

Inside, Bernard was pouring out a tirade of gratitude

that Felicity had introduced him to the most wonderful woman in the world, Caroline James.

'I am glad you are happy, Mr Anderson,' said Felicity. 'But please do rise and take a seat and tell me calmly what has happened. Are you engaged?'

'I have not dared ask her,' said Bernard. 'I have taken a job in the theater, you know.'

'No, of course I do not know. And what has Mrs Anderson to say to that?'

'She is furious, but there is nothing she can do,' said Bernard simply. 'Do you think there is hope for me with Miss James?'

'Mr Anderson, I really do not know. I have not seen Miss James since that day you met her. I am afraid you will need to ask her yourself.'

'I stayed the whole night with her,' said Bernard. He saw Felicity's raised eyebrows and blushed. 'I mean, I stayed all night and talked and talked. It was so wonderful.'

Outside on the staircase, the Marquess of Darkwater was finding to his irritation that his way was being barred by Agnes.

'Hush!' she said. 'They must not be disturbed.'

'What on earth are you babbling on about, you widgeon?' snapped the marquess. Agnes blushed painfully. His words and tone were like a bucket of cold water being thrown over her. The fantasy marquess of her dreams had a much better script.

'A Mr Anderson is proposing marriage to Felicity.'

'And did Miss Waverley order you from the room?'

'N-no, but you see . . .'

'He may prove to be another charlatan. You should not have left her.'

He mounted the stairs and opened the drawing room door. Bernard was now seated respectably in a chair with Felicity in a chair opposite. Felicity rose and curtsied and made the introductions.

The marquess looked from Bernard's glowing face to Felicity's amused one and said sharply, 'Well? Am I to congratulate you?'

'Why?' asked Felicity bluntly.

'I gather from Miss Joust you have just received a proposal of marriage.'

Agnes let out a faint bleating sound.

'If Miss Joust had stayed in the room,' said Felicity, 'she would have learned that Mr Anderson is indeed on the point of proposing to someone . . . but not to me.'

The marquess found he was feeling relieved but put it down to the fact that he was looking forward to the unraveling of the mystery about Felicity and did not want anyone else on the scene.

'I will bid you good day, Miss Waverley,' said Bernard. 'I pray you will come to my wedding.'

'Gladly,' said Felicity. 'Good luck!'

After he had left, the marquess asked curiously, 'What was all that about?'

'Mr Anderson is enamored of the actress Caroline James. He hopes to marry her.'

'A boy like that!'

'Miss James is very beautiful.'

'Granted. But there is a great difference in their ages.'

'Quite. Miss James is, I should guess, about your age, and Bernard, near to mine. Women marry older men every day. I do not see what is so wrong in that.'

'Women do not wear so well.'

'Only because they are worn out with childbirth,' said Felicity sharply.

'My dear Felicity!' cried Agnes. 'You must not say such things.'

The marquess turned and looked at his relative and then his eyes sharpened. 'I gather those are not your jewels, Miss Joust.'

'No, dear Felicity was kind enough to lend them to me.'

He turned back to Felicity. 'As for the Waverley jewels, do not trouble to sell any of them at the moment. I will pay all expenses, and we can settle our accounts later. I suggest we take them to my bank for safekeeping, and that includes those you have on, Miss Joust.'

Agnes's hand fluttered protectively to the necklace at her neck. 'Oh, but surely dear Felicity will need some for the journey.'

'I am grateful to you, my lord,' said Felicity. 'Those jewels have brought me nothing but trouble. But please do render me an exact account of all expenses when this adventure is over.'

'I have my carriage. I think we should take them to the bank now. If you do not mind, I shall send an item of news to the *Morning Post* to say the jewels are lodged in the bank. You do not want your servants to be imperiled.'

Felicity called Mrs Ricketts and two of the maids to help her carry the jewels downstairs. Her mind was working busily. She did not know what she thought of the marquess now, only that it was a relief to have some of her worries taken off her hands.

Agnes came with them to the bank and watched sulkily as all the jewels including the emerald necklace and bracelet were locked away in the vaults and Felicity tucked the receipt from the bank in her reticule. But soon a dream arose to console her. Felicity had been proved to be of low birth. The marquess came to rescue Agnes from her post as he had rescued her from Mrs Deves-Pereneux. As they drove away from Hanover Square, he handed her a flat morocco leather box, and when she opened it, there were the emeralds. 'I bought them for you, my beloved,' said the dream marquess. 'Poor Miss Waverley was only too glad to get the money for them. Of course, she cannot live in London any more now that the scandal of her birth is out. But we can, my darling, as man and wife.'

This was such a good dream, Agnes spent the rest of the day adding to it and embroidering it.

Felicity was already beginning to find this companion tiresome. She retired to her room early to prepare for the journey on the morrow. The marquess had proved not to be a villain. His only interest in her was as a provider of a mystery to amuse him. He had pointed out they were both heart-free. Felicity had often dreamed of having the company of some man as a friend. Now it seemed she had it. So why did she feel so low?

After some thought, she put it down to her dread at meeting Mrs Waverley again. She could never think of her as Baroness Meldon.

It was a blustery sunny morning when they set out for Meldon. The marquess's traveling carriage was comfortable and well-sprung. Felicity was tired after a night during which she had had little sleep and soon dozed off.

Agnes gazed hungrily at the marquess. She was sure he was longing for an opportunity to say something intimate to her. He was shy, of course. That was it. Since his wife's death, it was rumored he had shunned the company of the ladies. Perhaps he needed a little encouragement.

She smiled at him fondly and said, 'It is a fine day, is it not, Simon?'

The marquess looked at her coldly, and she blushed under his gaze. All at once, her use of his first name seemed like the impertinence it undoubtedly was. He took out a book and began to read.

Agnes could not bear the silence. After a little while, she gave a genteel cough and said tentatively, 'What are you reading, my lord?'

'*The Use of Phosphates in Increasing the Yield of Wheat*,' he said without raising his eyes.

'How interesting!' cried Agnes. 'I dote on phosphates.'

He raised his eyes. 'So you know about phosphates?'

'Yes, my lord. They are those pretty blue flowers, are they not?'

'Phosphates are salts that enrich the earth, like ferti-lizer,' he said. He lifted his book higher this time, as if to barricade himself from further questions.

'Silly me,' said Agnes with a tinkling laugh.

She did not feel at all stupid. A woman's role in life was to make a man feel superior on all occasions.

Felicity awoke and yawned and stretched. She blinked and looked around. Agnes put a playful finger to her lips. 'Shhh,' she admonished. 'Our gallant com-panion is deep in literature.'

'What are you reading?' Felicity asked curiously.

With an edge of irritation in his voice, the marquess told her.

'Oh,' said Felicity in surprise. 'Is that Hulm on phos-phates, or Jardine?'

He looked at her in amazement. 'Jardine, Miss Felicity. Never say you have read it.'

'Yes, indeed. Mrs Waverley considered a knowledge of the latest innovations in agriculture an essential part of my education.'

'You poor thing!' exclaimed Agnes.

'On the contrary, I found it fascinating. Is this to improve your plantations, my lord?'

'No, I own a small estate in Surrey that is not in good heart.'

The pair plunged into a long discussion on crops, phosphates, and drainage.

Agnes was just wondering whether it was possible to go into a decline through sheer boredom when a dream came to save her. The marquess was standing in the middle of a plowed field, hatless, shirt open at the neck, in leather breeches and thick shoes. She herself was wearing a simple peasant dress – lilac muslin, perhaps? – with one of those leather bodices. 'This land is all ours, my sweeting,' said the marquess, gathering her to his side with one hand and pointing across the field with the other. A warm wind blew Agnes's hair across her cheek, and he tenderly brushed it aside. She frowned in irritation. With his third hand? This dream needed more work. She resolutely closed her eyes. In no time at all, she was fast asleep.

The former Mrs Waverley, now Baroness Meldon, and her husband were dozing in front of the fire in the parlor after a hearty meal. The sound of carriage wheels crunching on the drive outside made both sit up.

'Callers,' said the baroness bitterly. In London, it was easy. If one did not want to be disturbed, then one's servant simply said one was not at home, but in the country, everyone for miles around seemed to know exactly when one was at home or out. 'I hope it is not the vicar,' she added. 'A most stupid and encroaching fellow.'

A footman came in carrying a card on a silver tray, which he presented to the baroness. The servants had quickly learned which one of the pair held the purse strings and managed the household.

The baroness fumbled for her quizzing glass and held it up scrutinizing the card. 'The Marquess of Darkwater,' she read. 'Don't know the man. What does he want, do you think?'

'Perhaps a friend of the Prince Regent,' said the baron importantly, brushing grains of snuff from his coat and straightening his wig.

'Show his lordship in,' said the baroness, getting to her feet.

The baron had turned away from the door and was arranging his crumpled cravat in the glass when he heard his wife's exclamation of dismay. He swung around. His eyes went straight past the marquess to where Felicity Waverley stood, and he turned a slightly muddy color.

Felicity had told the marquess she did not think their visit would be welcomed, but he had not expected them to be greeted with such shock and dismay.

The baroness wanted to forget all about the three girls she had adopted from the orphanage. The baron alone knew he had received his title from the Prince Regent on the understanding that he married Mrs Waverley and took her away from London. Why the Prince Regent should go to these lengths, the baron did not know, nor did he care. He had a title and a rich wife. Now, as he looked at Felicity, he dreaded that the prince would somehow learn of her visit and be displeased.

'Felicity,' said the baroness faintly. 'Why are you come?'

'May we sit down?' asked Felicity impatiently. 'We have journeyed from London to see you.'

'It is too small and stuffy here,' said the baroness with a distracted look about her. 'We will repair to the Green Saloon.'

The small party followed her across the hall and into a large, chilly, and very grand room. The baron had bought the house and estates with his wife's money. He loved his new home and he loved his title. Could the Prince Regent remove a title through displeasure?

The marquess sat down and looked at Baroness Meldon curiously. She was a massive stately woman like a figurehead on a ship. She looked at him, and she looked at Agnes, but she would not look at Felicity.

'We are come,' said Felicity, 'because I feel it is important to trace my parents.'

'But that is impossible,' said Mrs Waverley. 'And pointless. I gave you the jewels and the house. Why should you wreck your life by trying to find out about parents who were probably not even married?'

'Why should you believe that?' put in the marquess.

'They were charity cases at the orphanage,' said the baroness angrily. 'I gave them a home. I took them to my bosom. Did they thank me? Did they give me love? No!' She struck her breast. Agnes looked at her with approval. The baroness was behaving just as a lady ought.

'We are all grateful to you,' said Felicity. 'You know that. We might have loved you had you not kept us like prisoners in the house in Hanover Square. We might have loved you had you not tried to set us against one another.'

'Viper!' cried the baroness.

'In truth, Felicity, I must say you are too hard,' said Agnes.

'Do not interfere in matters that are not your

concern,' retorted Felicity. 'You must have some idea, ma'am. Why was it when Tredair tried to find out from the orphanage, they sent a messenger to warn you of his visit?'

'Because they considered it none of his concern.'

Felicity leaned forward. 'Then tell me, ma'am, why it is you turn faint when you see the Prince Regent and why his majesty looks most uncomfortable. Are we royal bastards?'

The baron exploded into wrath. 'Take yourselves off!' he shouted. 'Begone from my house and leave my wife in peace.' He rang the bell and told the footman who answered it, 'These persons are leaving. Have them escorted off the estate and make sure they are not allowed to return.'

The marquess was about to expostulate when he saw two letters lying open on a desk by the door. Felicity had got to her feet and was now raging at the baroness. He moved quietly to the door, straining his eyes to read the letters.

'You *unnatural* woman,' Felicity was saying. 'There is no need for this rudeness. And what of your famous principles? What of all your lectures on the evils of marriage?'

'Saints preserve us,' screamed the baroness. 'Am I to be molested in my own house, you strumpet? You came from the gutter, and you will no doubt return to the gutter when this fine lord has tired of you.'

'You have a mind like a kennel,' raged Felicity. 'What of your precious background?'

She found the marquess had taken her arm, and she

tried to shake him off. 'Come along, Miss Waverley,' he said. 'There is nothing for us here.'

The fight suddenly seemed to go out of her, and he led her from the room.

When they had gone, the baroness said, 'Ingratitude always makes me feel ill, my love. I am going to lie down.'

'I'll be up soon,' said the baron. 'Do not fret. I will make sure those tiresome people are not allowed to trouble you again. I must write an urgent letter.'

He sat for a long time at the writing desk. He did not particularly want to remind the Prince Regent of his existence, yet perhaps it might be better to tell him one of the Waverley girls was ferreting about. He bent his head and began to write.

The marquess found a comfortable inn to stay the night in the village of Meldon. He studied Felicity during supper. Agnes was prattling on, acting, as she fondly believed, the part of hostess and marchioness-to-be. Felicity, he thought, could do with a good cry. He wanted to tell her what he had found out but was reluctant to say anything in front of Agnes, who would cackle and exclaim. He regretted having chosen her to be a companion to Felicity, but, on the other hand, he was sorry for her, as he was sorry for all poor relations, neither fish nor fowl, treated with contempt by both servant and master. After they had finished the pudding and the covers had been removed, the marquess said, 'Miss Joust, I am sure you are tired and this business is really not your affair. Please leave us.'

Agnes bridled, and her long nose turned red. 'I feel it my duty to point out it is not at all the thing to leave Felicity unchaperoned.'

'We are in a public dining room, Miss Joust, not a private parlor. You force me to order you to leave us.'

Agnes got reluctantly to her feet. She dropped her fan and made a great work of picking it up. She then spent a long time arranging her shawl about her shoulders. At last, she left.

She stood outside the dining room, fretting. What were they talking about?

What if they were talking about *her*?

Then a rosy dream began to curl about her brain. They were talking about her. She could see the marquess, leaning back in his chair, toying with his glass of wine. 'Miss Waverley,' he was saying, 'I do hope all this is not too much for Miss Joust. My late wife was not strong, you know.' In the dream Felicity answered something or other. 'Yes,' the dream marquess went on, 'I worry about her. Will she be strong enough, for example, to endure the climate of the Indies?'

Agnes went out to stroll in the inn garden just in case he should care to come looking for her.

'I think I found something out,' said the marquess. 'Oh, cry, for heaven's sake. You will feel better.'

'I don't want to cry,' lied Felicity, although her eyes glistened with unshed tears.

'Then listen to this. While you were shouting at the baroness, I noticed two letters on the desk in the corner. One was a business letter from a firm of lawyers in Scarborough. I could not make out the rest.

There was no time, but enough to know it was about money and business. The lawyers are Baxter, Baxter, and Friend, Whitestairs Walk, Scarborough. If Mrs Waverley – I think of her as that, you know – if she has her business run from Scarborough, then that is probably where she came from. If we find out who exactly she is, where she was born, and who she married, we might have a clue as to your birth.'

'Scarborough,' said Felicity in a hollow voice.

'Yes, Scarborough. I suggest we return to London tomorrow and make preparations for the long journey.'

'You are very good, my lord,' said Felicity. 'I do not know why you should go to so much trouble on my behalf.'

'Because it amuses me,' he said with a smile.

And Felicity decided at that point that she really must escape to her bedchamber and burst into tears.

The marquess had said it would take two weeks to put his affairs in order and to make preparations for the long journey to Scarborough in Yorkshire.

Felicity found time lying very heavy on her hands. Agnes was beginning to irritate her immensely. She kept urging Felicity to take the Waverley jewels out of the bank – 'just for a little, you know. So terrible to think of them lying in a dusty vault where no one can see them.' Felicity protested wearily that the jewels should remain where they were until she returned from Scarborough. To escape from Agnes, she went to Covent Garden to see Caroline James. She was fortunate in finding the famous actress at home. Caroline welcomed her warmly and then listened in amazement as Felicity recounted her adventures at Meldon.

'So the third Waverley girl is to have a titled marriage,' teased Caroline.

Felicity looked surprised. 'What can you mean?'

'Why, this Lord Darkwater is going to a great deal of effort and expense on your behalf.'

'Oh, as to the effort, he says he is bored and the mystery amuses him, and as to the expense, I have promised to reimburse him.'

'Come now. There must be more to it than that.'

Felicity frowned. 'No. We have become friendly, that is all. I was mistaken in him. My first impression of him was wrong. He is a gentleman on all occasions and, believe me, there is nothing warmer in his attitude than that of friendship. But tell me about yourself? Mr Anderson called on me to tell me he had taken a job at the theater.'

'Yes, and a dreadful scene his mother made, too. I must confess, I thought the boy would soon tire, but he seems engrossed in his work and is very enthusiastic.'

'About his work – or about you?'

Caroline turned pink. 'It is calf love, nothing more. He will soon grow out of it.'

'And if he doesn't?'

'We'll see. I am much too old for him.'

'And yet the difference in your ages is almost the same as the difference in age between myself and Darkwater.'

'But that is not the same. Darkwater is a man.'

'What is that to do with it?'

'You must know you are being deliberately naive. This is a man's world, or had you forgot.'

'No, I am not likely to forget, particularly as I am burdened with a silly woman Darkwater has chosen to be my companion. But if one is of strong mind and independent spirit, then the conventions, most of them made by men, do not matter.'

'We'll see. How goes your writing?'

'Not at all. I appear to have run out of ideas.'

'With all the adventure in your life! Perhaps, like Miss Austen, you should base your writing on people and places you know well.'

'I do not find Miss Austen much of an inspiration,' said Felicity gloomily. 'Genius is never inspiring. I had better get back to Hanover Square before my companion drives my servants mad with her airs and graces.'

'Who is she?'

'A Miss Agnes Joust. A poor relation of Lord Darkwater. He rescued her from a tyrant of a mistress, but she does not seem in the least grateful to be with me.'

'Get rid of her!'

'I shall speak to Darkwater about her when we return from Scarborough.'

The Marquess of Darkwater walked through the gilded splendor of Clarence House. It was almost two weeks since he had been in Meldon. He found a letter from the Earl of Hopetoun waiting for him in which that peer angrily denied any knowledge of Colonel Macdonald.

The marquess had made all the necessary preparations for the journey north and planned to leave as
soon as possible. But before he could call at Hanover
Square to tell Felicity he was finally ready, he had
received a summons from the Prince Regent.

The Prince Regent was lying in a darkened saloon
on a chaise longue, wrapped in a Chinese dressing
gown with a turban made of cloth of gold on his head.

The marquess bowed and kissed the fat hand languidly extended in his direction.

'How may I be of service to you, Sire?' he asked.

'Hey, that's what we like in a man,' said the prince.
'Straight to the point with an offer of obedience and
duty.'

The marquess frowned. His offer had been a courtly
gesture, not to be taken seriously.

The prince propped himself up on one elbow. 'Sit
down, man, and take your ease. We have good news
for you.'

'Which is?' asked the marquess, pulling up a chair
beside the chaise longue and sitting down.

'We are leaving for Brighton tomorrow and wish
you to accompany us.'

'Sire, I am about to set out on a journey. I am flattered and pleased Your Majesty should wish my
company, but I must refuse.'

'You will obey your sovereign,' said the prince
wrathfully. 'We command you to accompany us to
Brighton.'

'Why?'

'What d'ye mean, why? Is our wish not enough?'

'In this case, Sire, no, it is not. Your Majesty has many friends and admirers to accompany you to Brighton.'

The prince looked more like a large cross baby than ever. He thought of the letter he had received from Meldon. He had decided to keep Darkwater with him in Brighton until such time as he considered the marquess had forgotten all about the Waverley girl. But perhaps he was worrying overmuch. Darkwater had an estate in Surrey. Perhaps he was bound there. Or, better still, back to the West Indies.

'Well, well, where are you bound that is so important?'

'Scarborough,' said the marquess.

'You shall not go. It does not please us.'

'May I ask why, Sire?'

'No, you may not,' roared the prince. 'Odd's fish, are we to account for our actions to every petty lord? Get out of our presence!'

The marquess rose and bowed and began to walk backward toward the door.

'Stay!' cried the prince. 'When do you set out?'

'In two days' time, Sire.'

The Prince Regent slumped down against the cushions and put a hand before his eyes. The marquess bowed his way out and shut the door behind him.

He drove straight to Hanover Square and told Felicity to make ready. They were leaving that very night.

Felicity exclaimed at the hastiness of the departure and demanded to know why. He replied he was bored and did not want to hang about London any longer. He did not want to scare her by telling her the real reason. He felt sure the prince would try to stop him. The secret to the royal distress lay in Scarborough and in the mysterious Mrs Waverley's background.

SIX

Felicity was never to forget that mad drive to the north of England. The marquess's traveling carriage pulled by six black horses moved at an amazing rate.

The marquess was driving his team himself. Agnes became so sick with the constant swaying motion that Felicity opened the trap in the roof and begged him to slow his pace because Agnes was ill. He called down heartlessly that if she looked like she was dying, he might consider stopping. Otherwise, he advised Miss Joust not to be sick in the carriage but to put her head out of the window.

'What did he say?' asked Agnes faintly.

'He is very concerned about you, but says that speed is of the uttermost importance,' lied Felicity.

A faint color came back to Agnes's wan cheeks. 'Dear Simon,' she murmured. 'So solicitous.'

Felicity was beginning to feel quite sick herself and

heaved a sigh of relief when they finally stopped at a posting house for the night.

The marquess opened the carriage door. Agnes collapsed into his arms and appeared to faint dead away.

'Was there ever such a woman?' he said crossly. 'Here, John,' he ordered one of the grooms, 'carry Miss Joust into the inn.'

Agnes felt herself being lifted in strong arms. She had been so busy pretending to be unconscious, she had not heard the marquess's order to his groom. She pretended to recover consciousness and wound her arms around John's neck and said, 'Oh, that this moment could last forever.'

She opened her eyes wide and gazed up into John's weatherbeaten face.

'Put me down, sir,' she cried, writhing like an eel. 'Where is your master?'

'Right behind, miss,' said John, tightening his hold. 'My lord said I am to carry you into the inn and carry you I shall.'

Furious, Agnes lay rigid like a plank, and like a plank, John propped her up against the wall of the hallway of the inn.

Agnes was furious. She had been nearly at death's door, and no one had cared. She would show them. She allowed Felicity to help her up the stairs to her room. One of the many things Agnes did not like about Felicity was that that self-sufficient young lady did not consider it necessary to employ the services of a maid. Agnes collapsed on the bed as Felicity efficiently ordered the chambermaids to unpack such items from their luggage as they would need for a night's stay at the inn.

Agnes was torn between pretending to be ill and staying in her room, or putting on her best lilac silk gown and dazzling the marquess. The lilac silk gown won the toss.

They had a private parlor. To Agnes's disappointment, the marquess was abstracted and said little. Felicity looked wan and tired, and he asked sharply, 'Are you sure you are fit to travel tomorrow, Miss Felicity? I am afraid our headlong dash has been a little too much for you.'

'And for poor me,' said Agnes pathetically.

He ignored her and looked at Felicity.

'I shall be well enough after a night's rest,' said Felicity. 'What of you, Agnes?'

'I suppose so,' said Agnes sulkily. Really, it was too bad of Simon. She was his flesh and blood and not some little parvenue of suspect birth like Felicity Waverley. What would he have done if she had been really ill? Agnes half closed her eyes. She could see in her mind's eye the darkened inn room and hear the hushed voices around the bed. 'I fear you may have been the cause of her grave malady, my lord,' the physician said. 'Ah, no, never say that!' cried the marquess, falling to his knees beside the bed. Agnes stretched out a hand as pale as alabaster to lightly touch his dark locks. 'I forgive you, Simon,' she whispered.

This scene was so very affecting that tears began to roll down Agnes's cheeks.

'Poor Agnes,' cried Felicity. 'It has all been too much

of a strain for you. Come and lie down, and I shall go to the kitchens myself and make you a posset.'

Agnes's agile brain raced. All at once, she had a plan in her mind, a plan that would get her the marquess's sympathy and might get Felicity accused of trying to murder her. Like some ladies of this first part of the nineteenth century, Agnes took a small quantity of arsenic to add luster to her hair and to keep her skin clear. She had enough of the poison with her to ensure she would be very sick but in no danger. She would put the arsenic in the posset Felicity brought her and then say she had been poisoned.

'Thank you my dear,' she said faintly. 'That would be most welcome.'

Felicity took her up to her room, helped her undress, and put her to bed. She then went back to the parlor to say good night to the marquess.

He gave her a rueful smile. 'I engaged Miss Joust to look after you. I am afraid she is not a suitable companion.'

But Agnes's plight had touched Felicity's kind heart. 'She means well,' she said. 'The journey was a hectic dash. Is such speed really necessary?'

'Yes.'

'But why?'

'If Mrs Waverley has something to hide, she may have written to Scarborough to alert her lawyers.'

Felicity shook her head in bewilderment. 'She has no reason to know we are bound for Scarborough.'

'She may have guessed. It is better we reach there as fast as possible.'

'Very well,' said Felicity reluctantly. 'I only hope Agnes manages to get a good night's sleep. At what hour do we depart in the morning?'

'Six o'clock.'

Felicity groaned.

She made her way to the kitchens and ordered the cook to produce the necessary materials for a posset, made it up, and carried it in a cup on a tray to Agnes's room. Agnes was lying in bed with her eyes half closed. Felicity noticed with surprise that Agnes's hair was still piled on top of her head and that her lips were slightly rouged. She did not know Agnes had prepared for her famous deathbed scene.

'Dear Felicity,' said Agnes. 'Leave it beside me.'

'Would you like me to stay with you until you fall asleep?' asked Felicity.

'No, Felicity, I shall do very well.' Agnes waited until Felicity had gone and then climbed from her bed and found the paper twist of arsenic she carried in her reticule. She carefully measured some grains into the cup. She knew she was going to have an uncomfortable time of it, but was sure she had not put in enough to make her actually vomit.

But Agnes had misjudged the dose. Felicity's room was next door, and she was aroused in the night by Agnes's screams for help.

She ran next door. The room reeked of vomit, and Agnes was standing, clutching her throat. 'Poison,' she screamed. 'Poison.'

The noise alerted the marquess. He took one look at the situation and called for the inn servants. Soon a glass was pressed into Agnes's hand, and his stern voice was commanding her to drink it. She threw the contents down her throat as the marquess seized the chamber pot and stood at the ready. Agnes spluttered, and her eyes bulged. It had been hot water liberally laced with rock salt.

Agnes was dreadfully sick. But by the time the physician arrived, she was lying weak and pale in the bed, purged of all the poison, and able to start to accuse Felicity. 'I think it was that posset,' she said faintly. 'See, you may examine it. There is a little in the cup.'

The physician was a dour Scotsman who had been roused from his bed. 'It certainly appears to be some sort of poisoning,' he said, and Agnes closed her eyes in satisfaction. But his next words were not at all what she had expected. The doctor was examining the contents of the toilet table. He then picked up Agnes's reticule and said, 'Mind if I look in here, my lord?' and then without waiting for permission, he drew open the strings of the reticule and tipped the contents out on the table.

He picked up the twist of paper, gently opened it, and carried it over to the oil lamp to examine the contents. 'Arsenic,' he said, his face grim. 'These silly women, playing with death. They will do it.'

'That is not mine,' cried Agnes. 'I do not know how it got there!'

And then came the marquess's voice, as cold as ice. 'If you are suggesting Miss Felicity put some in that posset and put the rest in your reticule, Miss Joust, then I suggest you recover as quickly as possible and find your own way back to London.'

The physician came to the bed holding the oil lamp and peered down at Agnes. 'I thought so,' he said. 'Do you see those moles, my lord? Here, and here?' He pointed to a mole on Agnes's chin and then one on her forehead. 'An arsenic eater, quite definitely.'

'Was a man ever plagued by such a dangerously silly woman?' said the marquess furiously. 'Well, Miss Felicity? Shall we continue on our journey and leave her behind?'

Agnes burst into frightened tears. 'I am sorry, Felicity. It was wicked and silly of me. Yes, I do occasionally take arsenic and was ashamed to confess to the practice.' Tears poured down her cheeks.

'It is all right,' said Felicity. 'No one is going to send you away. My lord, we cannot travel tomorrow.'

He looked furious, and then suddenly his face relaxed. 'Very well,' he murmured. 'It might be interesting to see what happens. I may be worrying overmuch.'

Agnes was genuinely weak and ill the next day. At one point, she managed to struggle from the bed and look out the window. Her window overlooked the inn garden, and the sight that met her eyes did little to cheer her. It was a fine, sunny, very English afternoon. A light wind was pushing great fleecy clouds across a blue sky. The sun shimmered on the winding river bordering the inn garden. Walking along the riverbank was the Marquess of Darkwater and Miss

Felicity Waverley. Felicity was wearing a lilac muslin gown – *my* color, thought Agnes, gritting her teeth. It was high-waisted and had long tight sleeves ending in points at the wrist. It had a little gauze ruff at the neck and three deep flounces at the hem. Under the hem, little lilac kid shoes peeped in and out. On her head was one of the new transparent hats, a circle of stiffened gauze decorated with white flowers. The lilac gown, like the matching parasol she carried, was ornamented with a little white spot.

The marquess was in morning dress: blue coat, striped waistcoat, pantaloons, and Hessian boots. He was laughing at something Felicity was saying, and she was smiling up at him. Agnes got back into bed and rang the bell.

When a chambermaid came in, Agnes groaned pathetically and said, 'Fetch Miss Waverley. I am nigh to death.'

The minute the chambermaid had left, Agnes got up again and looked down from the window. Soon the chambermaid appeared below, the streamers of her cap flying. She stopped before the couple and began to talk. Felicity looked startled and made a move to leave, but the marquess placed a hand on her arm to restrain her and said something to the chambermaid. Agnes crawled back into bed and practiced a few groans. She waited and waited. At last the door opened, and, to her horror, neither Felicity nor the marquess appeared but the crusty Scottish doctor, who gave her a draft of something, told her to behave herself and stop wasting his time, and left. It was shortly after he had gone that Agnes realized he had given her a heavy sleeping draft, the doctor having put her down as a hysterical woman who needed sedation. So when Felicity did look in, Agnes was sleeping peacefully. She returned to the garden to tell the marquess the news, and found him in the company of two gentlemen. Felicity was versed enough in the ways of the world to recognize such men as gentlemen when she saw them, although the less initiated might have assumed that men attired in many-caped coats despite the warmth of the day and wearing belcher neckcloths belonged to the stables. Here then were two Corinthians with clothes and manners to match.

'Who's the filly, Darkwater?' asked one as Felicity approached them.

'That is Miss Waverley,' said the marquess, 'and if either of you refer to her as a filly again, I shall take great pleasure in ramming your teeth down your throat. Miss Felicity,' he said, as she reached them, 'allow me to present Sir George Comfrey and Mr Peter Harris.'

'Pleasure,' said Mr Harris laconically. He did not remove the straw he had been chewing from his mouth. He was a squat, brutal-looking man with blue jowls and broken teeth. Sir George Comfrey was tall and thin with a long nose and slanting pale green eyes. He looked like a fox.

He made an elaborate bow.

'What brings you here, Harris?' asked the marquess.

'Same as yourself,' said Mr Harris. 'Traveling north. Stay with m'friend in Harrogate. When do you leave?'

'It depends on the health of Miss Waverley's companion. She was taken ill last night. Hopefully we might be able to leave tomorrow.'

'You said you were bound for Scarborough? What takes you there, Darkwater?'

'I am going there on business of a private nature.'

There was a little silence. Both men exchanged glances. Felicity wished they would leave. It had been so comfortable walking in the garden with the marquess and talking about all sorts of things. 'Care to broach a few bottles in the tap?' asked Comfrey.

'No,' said the marquess pleasantly. 'I prefer the company of Miss Waverley.'

The two men began to move reluctantly away.

'Are they friends of yours?' asked Felicity.

'No, mere acquaintances. The darker side of Prinny's entourage, I think.'

Felicity looked shocked. 'I do not think our Prince Regent would relish the company of such fellows. Forgive me for speaking plain, my lord, but I could not like them.'

'Then we shall avoid them. There are always such characters on the fringes of the court. Sporting is all the rage, and quite a number of men wish to look and sound like a cross between their own coachmen and gallows birds.'

Agnes joined them for dinner that evening. The deep sleep had refreshed her, and she wanly declared she felt quite her normal self. Felicity insisted they should stay one more day to make absolutely sure Agnes did not have a relapse. The marquess frowned impatiently but said nothing. He felt uneasy about the sudden appearance of two of Prinny's toadies.

He did not see what those two could do to stop their journey north, if such was their intention. He posted two of his grooms in the passageway outside their rooms with instructions to rouse him at the slightest sign of anyone approaching.

The marquess found it hard to get to sleep. He tried to remember his wife as she had been when he was courting her and to remember if he had felt the easy companionship in her company he had enjoyed with Felicity in the inn garden. But all he could remember was it had been a strict and correct courtship and he had not really been alone with her until their wedding night. He closed his eyes in pain as he remembered that night. How she had writhed away from him and called him a monstrous cruel and unfeeling brute. After that miserable night, she had complained of headaches and backaches and every kind of malaise. He was sure she was making every excuse she could think of not to sleep with him. Although he had tried to cherish her, to treat her with tenderness, she had infinitely preferred the company of her lady's maid. He had been most surprised when she had died, to find she really had been a frail creature, yet he had nothing with which to reproach himself. Before he met Felicity Waverley, he had never before envisaged a woman as being a friend and companion.

He was just about to slip off gently into sleep at last when a voice in his brain asked, What would *you* do if you wanted to stop three people journeying north?

'I would wreck their carriage,' he answered crossly in his mind. All at once, he sat bolt upright. The carriage!

Felicity, too, was awake. She could not stop thinking about the marquess. She turned over and over in her mind everything they had said that day. She thought of the charm of his deep voice, of the humorous twist to his mouth, and of the way his normally cold gray eyes had lit up with laughter as he had looked down at her. But there was something about this journey and the frantic need for haste that he had not told her. And what of those two ugly men, Harris and Comfrey?

And then she heard a low voice in the passage outside. She ran to the door, unlocked it, and looked out. The marquess was talking to his groom. He looked up when he saw Felicity and said sharply, 'Get back to bed.'

'Where are you going?' she asked softly.

'Just as far as the stables to see that everything is all right.'

She closed the door, but stood irresolute. The stables. All at once she did not like the idea of his going out in the blackness of the night with Harris and Comfrey possibly around.

Feeling silly, but determined to go ahead with it, she opened her trunk and took out a small pistol and primed it. Then she pulled a warm cloak with a hood over her nightgown and slipped her bare feet into a soft pair of kid shoes. She made her way swiftly out into the passage and down the stairs. The inn door was standing open. Outside, a high wind was blowing, and a small bright moon was racing through the clouds. The stables were at the back of the inn. She felt in her pocket for the cold reassuring smoothness of her pistol and hurried across the yard.

The marquess had checked the horses. All was well. He made his way through to the carriage house, moving as silently as a ghost. Just as silently, the groom crept behind him.

All appeared to be quiet and still, yet there was an atmosphere of danger in the air. The wind sighed around the building and pieces of straw drifted across the floor. The carriage gleamed softly in a shaft of pale moonlight coming in through a high barred window at the end. Feeling confident now that he had been imagining things, he strode forward. And then a sickening blow struck him from behind and, as he went down, he could hear a groan behind him from the groom, who had also been attacked.

He lay on the cobbles fighting to keep conscious while the whole world seemed to whirl about him.

'Right, Comfrey,' said Harris. 'Bring that ax over here. A few blows on the wheels of this carriage should be enough, and then we'll be on our way.'

Slowly the marquess eased himself up onto one elbow and shook his head to clear it. Harris was standing by the gleaming panels of the coach, an ax in his hand. He raised it to bring it down on the wheels when a clear feminine voice called out, 'Hold hard, or I shall blow your brains out!'

Harris dropped the ax and he and Comfrey swung

around to face the doorway. Felicity Waverley stood there, a small pistol in her hand.

Comfrey began to laugh. 'Pick up the ax, man,' he said to Harris. 'She ain't going to do anything with that toy.'

Harris bent down to pick up the ax and a bullet whizzed through his hat. He stayed where he was in a half crouch as if frozen. The marquess struggled to his feet. Felicity was reloading her pistol. 'Are you unhurt, my lord?' she called.

'Yes,' he said, moving toward the two men.

'Do not get between me and the line of fire, my lord,' said Felicity coolly.

The marquess nodded and unhitched a coil of rope from the wall. Stumbling slightly, for he still felt groggy, he tied up the two men. 'It was only a joke, Darkwater,' pleaded Comfrey. 'See here, did it for a wager, don't you know?'

'You can explain matters to the justice of the peace,' said the marquess. His groom groaned and shifted. He went and bent over him and then felt his pulse. The landlord of the inn came running in followed by some of his servants.

'These men tried to wreck my carriage after attacking me and my groom,' said the marquess. 'Call the constable and have them taken to the roundhouse for the night.'

He waited until Harris and Comfrey had been bundled out and then went to Felicity. 'Where did you learn to shoot like that?'

'Mrs Waverley taught me,' said Felicity.

'What an extraordinary woman,' he said with a grin. 'Finding out about her past is going to be a pleasure.'

'Are you badly hurt?' she asked.

'My head is quite hard, but I must confess I feel pretty sick.'

The landlord came back with more servants, and the groom was carried out. Instructions were given to rouse the Scottish doctor from his bed again to attend to the groom.

'And now,' said the marquess, 'back to bed, Miss Felicity. We will go to the authorities in the morning and find out what these two ruffians have to say for themselves.'

'There is something wicked about this,' said Felicity with a shiver. 'Someone is very anxious to stop us from finding out about Mrs Waverley.'

She looked white and strained. He had a longing to take her in his arms, but prudence held him back. He was not sure of his feelings. And then at the back of his mind, he was always haunted by the coldness of his wife.

'They were probably doing it for a wager,' he said, although he didn't believe it. 'Come along, Miss Felicity.'

They made their way out. The inn was ablaze with lights and the courtyard full of guests demanding to know what had happened.

Felicity was glad to escape to her room. She had a longing to tell him she had changed her mind, that she did not want to find out anything about Mrs Waverley. Her dull existence in Hanover Square now seemed like paradise. What was she doing risking her life on the Great North Road when she had a comfortable home and the efficient Mrs Ricketts to take care of everything?

Agnes was furious to learn she had slept through all the excitement. She eagerly asked Felicity to repeat over and over again what had happened. Agnes was bitterly jealous. Knowing how to prime and fire a pistol was a most unmaidenly talent, yet she wished she had been the one to save the marquess.

They were sitting in the private parlor having a late breakfast when the marquess came in, looking grim. 'They've gone,' he said, sitting down at the end of the table.

'Harris and Comfrey?' exclaimed Felicity. 'How can that be? They were surely locked up in the roundhouse.'

'They were visited during the night by the local justice of the peace, Mr Haggerty. I roused Mr Haggerty and demanded an explanation. He is a weak, shiftless man. He began to bluster that the two criminals were fine gentlemen who had only been playing a prank. I swore and said I had been struck nigh unconscious and my groom attacked as well, that they had been on the point of wrecking my carriage. He apologized but said he was sure a fine gentleman like myself would not wish to press charges. I said I most certainly did, and he said he would send men out to look for the pair.' He fell silent, wondering again if the pair had used the magic of the Prince Regent's name to escape.

Agnes shivered. 'They may come back and attack us!'

'I doubt it,' said the marquess, but he added silently, But someone else may.

Agnes wanted to continue to play the ailing invalid, but the thought that if they waited any longer at the inn they might be attacked by Harris and Comfrey decided her against it.

The little party set out again at dawn the next day. Agnes could not help noticing that the marquess's attitude to Felicity had noticeably changed. Before he had always been courteous and polite. But now there was a warmth in his smile and admiration in his eyes when he looked at her.

Blowsy strumpet! thought Agnes furiously. She would come to a bad end like her sisters, or not her sisters, but those other two. Then Agnes realized for the first time that she did not know what had happened to the other two. Before her job with Mrs Deves-Pereneux, she had been taking care of an elderly lady in the country and so had not heard much town gossip. Agnes did not read the newspapers either, or she would have learned of the adventures of the famous Waverleys.

'Do you ever hear from the other two ladies?' she asked.

'Who?' Felicity was looking dreamily out the window.

'I mean the other two ladies who were adopted with you. I gather they do not reside with you any more.'

'Oh, Fanny and Frederica? They are married.'

Of course they are, thought Agnes. Mrs Waverley, who could buy all those fabulous jewels, had no doubt bought them lowly but honest husbands.

'And where are they now?' asked Agnes.

'Both are still on the Continent, I believe,' said Felicity. 'Fanny, Lady Tredair, is now in Paris, and Frederica, Lady Harry Danger, is in Rome. Goodness, how tired I am, but it is hard to get any rest with the sickening motion of this carriage.'

'Mrs Waverley, or rather, Baroness Meldon, no doubt worked hard to secure such good husbands,' said Agnes, who had hardly been able to believe her ears at the sound of both titles.

'On the contrary, she worked very hard to stop either of them marrying. Both married without even a dowry.'

For one brief anguished moment, a flash of common sense penetrated Agnes's mind, a mind normally cobwebbed by dreams and fantasies. Such was the power and attraction of the Waverley girls that neither birth nor lack of dowry had stopped two of them from marrying the best in the land. She, Agnes, should appreciate that she was well-treated as a companion and strive to hold this post for as long as possible.

But jealousy combined with fantasy soon took over again. The marquess's voice seemed to sound in her ears. He was confiding to Agnes his worries about Felicity. 'As soon as I saw her waving that pistol about, Miss Joust,' he was saying, 'I knew she could not be of gentle birth. No lady even knows one end of a pistol from the other.'

So Agnes's dreams grew stronger as the miles and days flew past and the air grew colder and fresher and was tinged with the salt of the sea.

At long last, the marquess's voice from the box shouted down, 'Scarborough!'

Felicity tugged at the strap and let down the glass and leaned out. Cliffs and elegant buildings and a magnificent stretch of blue sea and an odd feeling of recognition and familiarity braced the Yorkshire air.

Somehow she knew the long journey to find the identity of her parents was nearly over.

SEVEN

The seaside of the aristocracy had grown from the fashion for visiting spas. The move from inland spa to seaside had been gradual. It had begun at Scarborough, where a mineral spring by the seashore had first attracted visitors to the town. Some enthusiasts had bathed there in the seventeenth century when the government had even considered taxing bathers on the grounds that the seas belonged to the kings of England. At that time, a few aristocrats sporting naked in the sea had not been enough to make Scarborough fashionable. The impetus started in the middle of the eighteenth century when Dr Richard Russell set about promoting the use of seawater to cure disease – taken internally. According to Russell, seawater in half-pint doses, mixed if necessary with port or milk, could cure scurvy, jaundice, gonorrhea, gout, and other ailments.

The fashion for seaside holidays having been

established, the visitors set about creating the same atmosphere that prevailed at the inland spas. Assembly rooms were built, establishments for taking the waters and bathing in them were set up by doctors and professors of the new science, reading rooms were built at which card games and raffles were included among the amusements, and every social event was designed to provide a medium for getting to know other visitors.

The marquess was anxious to go to the lawyers as soon as possible before the news of their arrival was published in the social columns of the local papers. He obviously did not consider Scarborough a very safe place for them to reside in for very long, thought Felicity wistfully, as she stood on the balcony of her hotel room and looked out across the sea. It was such a jolly place, and the changing colors of the sea were fascinating.

And then a tall man came into view, walking along the esplanade in front of the hotel. He was holding onto his hat. He sported a fine pair of black military sideburns. There was something about his manner, and the confident air of the man, that forcibly reminded Felicity of Colonel Macdonald. The man looked up and saw the slight figure on the balcony. He tugged his hat down over his eyes and went on his way, his pace a little faster than before.

Colonel Macdonald, now the Comte D'Angiers, his Irish brogue changed to a lisping French accent, hurried on his way. When he had gone some distance, he turned about and looked back at the hotel. The figure on the balcony had gone, but he had recognized Felicity Waverley. He thought of those jewels and his mouth watered like that of a hungry man thinking of a sumptuous banquet. He had done well at cards at the gaming tables of Scarborough and was feted and petted by the ladies and had as many social invitations as he could desire. But he wanted to secure enough money to end his shaky life of cheating and lying.

He slowly turned about and made his way back to the hotel. He reminded himself that with his hair dyed and his new Frenchified air, Felicity would hardly recognize him unless he got too close.

He hesitated outside the hotel, then squared his shoulders and strolled inside. The manager came forward to welcome him. The comte was a prime attraction with the ladies, and his presence in the hotel usually meant extra guests for tea and other refreshments.

'Any new guests, m'sieur?' drawled the comte.

'Yes,' said the manager importantly. 'The Marquess of Darkwater.'

The comte frowned and half turned, about to escape. But perhaps his eyes had been deceiving him. 'Did he come with a party, or alone?'

'His Lordship came with a most beautiful young lady, a Miss Waverley, and her companion, Miss Joust. Why, I believe that is His Lordship coming down the stairs.'

The soi-disant comte moved behind the screen of a potted palm and looked through its fronds. It was indeed the marquess and Felicity. He watched as they exchanged a few pleasantries with the manager. Then they went outside and walked off along the esplanade.

He moved out from the shelter of the palm and approached the manager again. 'I see no sign of the companion,' he said.

'Probably in her room,' said the manager. The comte thought quickly. Companions were poor sorts of creatures, easily gulled. 'I seem to remember meeting a Miss Joust in London,' he said. 'Perhaps you could present my card and ask her if she would do me the honor of taking tea with me on the terrace?'

The manager bowed, took the card, and hurried off. The comte made his way to the terrace, which, in fact, was a long narrow room with French windows overlooking the sea. It was not the fashionable hour for tea, so there were few people about.

Agnes had been moping in her room when the comte's invitation was delivered to her. She had been feeling very low at being left behind by the marquess, but the marquess had begun to think the less Miss Joust knew of Felicity's affairs the better. He had put her down as an unstable, gossipy woman.

She did not stop to consider that she had never met any French comte in London. Excited and elated at the invitation, she dressed in her best lilac gown, ran to Felicity's room and borrowed a handsome cashmere shawl, and then made her way downstairs to the terrace.

That the comte must indeed know her appeared to be borne out by the fact that he rose and bowed as soon as she entered the room. But the comte, looking at the long-nosed dab of a creature, knew immediately this must be Miss Joust. Companions were always stamped with the mark of faded gentility.

As she came up to him, he seized her hand and kissed it, clicking his heels together.

'I am enchanted to meet you again,' he said.

Agnes blushed and simpered. He held out a chair for her, then snapped his fingers. The comte ordered tea and cakes, then sat down next to Agnes.

'I have been trying to recall where we met, my lord,' said Agnes.

'Sure . . .' he began, then remembered in time he was supposed to be French, not Irish. '*Ma foi*, Miss Joust,' he said. 'I have a terrible confession to make. We have not met.'

'Indeed!'

'I saw you driving out with Miss Waverley, and I made it my business to know who you were.'

This was like one of Agnes's very best fantasies. That she had only been companion to Felicity for a very short time and how truly amazing it was that the comte should have had a chance to see her in London and then miraculously appear so quickly in Scarborough did not enter her mind. She threw him a killing glance, and he looked suitably smitten, as though by Cupid's arrow.

He began to ask her what they were doing in Scarborough, and Agnes looked down her long nose and said it was all very mysterious and dear Simon would be furious with her if she told anyone.

'Simon?'

'The marquess is my cousin.'

'If you are a cousin to a *marquis*,' exclaimed the comte, 'I am *bouleversé* that he should allow you to work as a companion to such an eccentric young lady.'

'He did not want me to, of course,' said Agnes. 'But I prefer to earn my keep rather than be anyone's pensioner.' Agnes was not surprised to hear Felicity described as eccentric. Young ladies who carried pistols and knew how to use them were eccentric in the extreme.

'Most commendable. But an onerous task, considering the dangers attached to it.'

'Dangers?'

'I assume Miss Waverley has all her famous jewels with her. Attempts have been made before to steal them.'

'No,' said Agnes crossly, thinking of that dear emerald necklace. 'She lodged them all in Simon's bank before we left.'

The comte nearly rose to his feet and left there and then. But apart from his desire to get his hands on the jewels, he also wanted revenge on Felicity. He remembered her masquerade as Miss Callow and how her disguise had slipped when she had kicked him in the stomach. He had decided she had deliberately disguised herself and lured him to her home with a promise that he would be able to sell the jewels for her, only to unmask him.

Then he heard Agnes complain, 'So silly to lock all the jewels away and not even take a few trinkets for the journey. Yet she leaves the bank receipt for the jewels lying about where anyone might pick it up.'

The comte let out a slow breath. He was glad the waiter arrived at that moment with the tea things, for his excitement was so great, he felt it must show on his face.

He did not immediately return to the matter of the jewels. He encouraged Agnes to talk and quickly learned that she was in love with the marquess and was bitterly jealous of Felicity and that she coveted those jewels almost as much as he did himself.

He slid in little barbed remarks. It was a pity one so fair as Miss Joust should have to wait hand and foot on a lady of doubtful background. Then he flattered her. Did she know lilac was her color and she should never wear anything else? Did she know her eyes were like moonstones? And Agnes's eyes shone like pale oysters in a barrel of dough, and her yearnings for the marquess dimmed and faded to be replaced by yearnings for this handsome comte.

'It is a sad life being a companion,' said Agnes, 'and also dangerous.'

'How so?'

'I shall tell you this in confidence. May I trust you?'

'Word of a D'Angiers,' he said, putting his hand on his heart.

Agnes leaned forward and looked to the right and left. Then she said slowly, 'On the journey north, Felicity tried to poison me.'

Mad, quite mad, thought the comte. But he exclaimed in horror and begged for more details.

'Simon had been paying me . . . well, extra attention. He is, how shall I say, a little bit overwarm in his attentions to me. Felicity noticed. I was sick from the mad pace at which we were traveling, and she offered to make me a posset. She laced it with arsenic! Had not Simon heard my cries and given me an emetic, I should most certainly have died.'

'But milord, the marquess, did he do nothing to have her brought to justice?'

'She! She made sheep's eyes at him, and then she bribed a savage Scottish doctor to say I was an arsenic-eater.'

The comte correctly interpreted all this to mean that Agnes was an arsenic-eater, had tried to bring disgrace on Felicity, and had overdone things and been unmasked. He had a weak pang of sympathy for Felicity. What a fright this woman was!

But the afternoon wore on as he charmed and flattered, and when he finally begged Agnes not to reveal their meeting, Agnes readily agreed, although she would not for one moment admit to herself the real reason for complying with the request, which was fear this comte should fall in love with Felicity if he set eyes on her.

He got her to agree to slip out that evening after Felicity had gone to bed and to take a walk with him in the moonlight. Agnes felt it was the happiest moment of her life.

The marquess and Felicity sat facing Mr Baxter, the senior partner of Baxter, Baxter, and Friend. He repeated that Baroness Meldon owned some property in Scarborough that she rented out and that her main business affairs were handled by a firm in the city of London. He did not know anything of the baroness's background and implied that if he did, he would not reveal it.

When the marquess and Felicity finally took their leave, Felicity asked, 'Do you think he was warned of our arrival?'

The marquess shook his head. 'He was behaving just like any ordinary provincial lawyer. But why should she buy property in Scarborough if she has no connection with the place? I wonder where it is.'

'He would not even tell us that,' pointed out Felicity.

'But somewhere in that musty office is a box, which, I feel sure, would tell us a lot more. Leave it to me.'

'What are you going to do?'

'Break in after nightfall.'

'That will not answer,' said Felicity practically. 'When he returns in the morning and finds the shattered door, we will be the first suspects.'

'He will not find anything out of order,' said the marquess. 'I managed to get hold of a set of these before I left London.' He drew a ring of skeleton keys from his pocket.

'Let me come with you,' said Felicity eagerly.

'No, stay and get some rest.'

He remained resolutely deaf to her protests. 'And do not breathe a word of my plans to Miss Joust. She is a good-hearted lady but silly and gossipy.'

Felicity had long ago come to the conclusion that Agnes was not good-hearted in the slightest, yet she felt a great pity for her. Felicity was firmly convinced all women had such a hard role to play in life, it was no wonder they turned out such poor creatures. She could not find it in her heart to blame Agnes for her silliness. She thought Agnes had poisoned herself not to try to get her, Felicity, accused of murder, but simply to draw attention to herself. Also Felicity had gradually realized that Agnes was in love with the marquess, and that awareness had made her treat her companion with more kindness than she deserved.

Felicity decided to spend the evening after dinner being pleasant to Agnes. But she had become so used to London hours, she had forgotten dinner would be served at four in the afternoon. Agnes, because she had stayed on the terrace with the comte, had missed dinner, too, but declared wanly she could not eat a thing and would go to bed early.

The marquess ordered a late supper for himself and Felicity, late for the hotel, but at the London hour of seven in the evening.

He was abstracted and talked little. Felicity began to worry that he was becoming bored with the whole affair.

When dinner was over, he asked her to lock the door of her room and to make sure Miss Joust kept her door locked as well.

Felicity went to Agnes's room. She knocked at the door but did not receive any reply. She tried the handle, but the door was locked. Assuming Agnes had gone to bed, Felicity sighed with relief. She would have the rest of the evening to herself.

But she did not want to stay confined in her room. It

would be pleasant to go down to the terrace and drink coffee and listen to the sound of the sea. When she reached the terrace, she wondered at the propriety of what she was doing. She really should not be unchaperoned. But the tables in the terrace room were empty except for four old ladies drinking negus and eating sweet biscuits.

They all bowed as Felicity passed, and Felicity dropped them a low curtsy and sat at the table next to theirs.

She was soon to know they had all learned her name. Addressing her as Miss Waverley, they introduced themselves. The spokeswoman for the group was a Mrs Crabtree. 'Do you and Lord Darkwater plan to stay in Scarborough long?' she asked.

'Not very long,' said Felicity.

'Not on holiday, then?' asked Mrs Crabtree after much whispering.

'Yes, in a way,' said Felicity, wishing she had sat at another table.

More whispering transpired and then Mrs Crabtree asked, 'You come from London?'

'Yes, ma'am.'

'Ah, the dear Season. I wonder you can bear to leave it. Does the Prince Regent attend many functions?'

'Yes, Mrs Crabtree. His Royal Highness enjoys parties as much as ever.'

'How beautiful he was as a young man,' sighed Mrs Crabtree. And 'Beautiful . . . beautiful . . .' murmured her friends in a sort of Greek chorus. 'Our young Prince Florizel. We were all in love with him.'

One thin lady leaned forward and muttered fiercely in Mrs Crabtree's ear.

'Yes, but she don't want to know about a scandal like that,' said Mrs Crabtree. She smiled at Felicity. 'Old gossip. One of our dashing young matrons set her cap at the prince all those years ago. Her poor husband. Such a to-do.'

Felicity sat up straight, her eyes suddenly shining with excitement. 'Was this matron's name Waverley, Mrs Waverley?'

'No, no.' Mrs Crabtree shook her head, and the Whitby jet ornaments on her cap glittered in the lamplight. 'It wasn't that. Now, what was it?' The ladies put their heads together and whispered and muttered, but not one of them could remember the name. 'She wasn't from here,' explained Mrs Crabtree. 'York, I believe.'

The marquess sat at the desk in the lawyer's office going through a pile of receipts and books and papers. They were all connected with three buildings in Cliff Place East. The lawyers had records of having received money for the rentals and then of sending bank drafts to Mrs Waverley at Hanover Square and then, more recently, to Baroness Meldon at Meldon. The marquess took a note of the address. The office contained no other clue. He could only hope there was some elderly resident in one of the properties who remembered Mrs Waverley.

He put everything back in place, glad that the office, unlike most lawyers' offices, was so well-dusted. That meant he did not have to worry about leaving smears and fingerprints.

Having spent a long time finding the right key on the ring to open the office door, he was able to close it quickly and make his escape. Although it was early in the evening, the town streets were deserted. The residents went to bed early. Only the fashionable, elderly dowagers and visitors stayed up late in the hotels.

He was walking along the blackness of the esplanade when he nearly collided with an amorous couple who were locked in each other's arms. He muttered an apology, swerved, and went on his way.

'That was Darkwater!' cried Agnes. 'Did he see us?'

'No,' said the comte. 'He did not, my darling.'

'Oh, then, kiss me again,' said Agnes.

'I cannot,' said the comte, who had had more than enough of Agnes. 'I fear I could not restrain my passions. Oh, that we could be wed!'

For once in her life, Agnes very nearly fainted – such was her emotion on hearing those beautiful words.

'But why can't we marry?' she asked, pressing close to him.

'I am a poor man. I lost all my fortune. My parents were guillotined, and I was brought to England as a young boy. I have my wits and talents and a certain skill with cards, but I could not ask any lady, especially one of gentle birth and sensibility such as yourself, to share my vagabond life.'

'Take me!' said Agnes, throwing her head back. 'We will wander the roads of England together, like gypsies, stealing an occasional crust of bread and living on berries.'

He sighed. 'It does seem an unfair life when such as Felicity Waverley has a fortune in jewels and thinks so little of them that she leaves them to molder unseen in some bank vault. No! Forget I ever spoke of marriage. It is impossible.'

He waited hopefully in the darkness. How long would it take the silly bitch's mind to work it out?

'I could take that receipt for the jewels,' said Agnes at last. 'We could collect the jewels and flee the country.'

He almost laughed with relief. But instead he said passionately, 'I cannot expose you to such danger. Come, I will kiss you one last time.'

Agnes, dizzy with passion and mad with hope, spent quite half an hour persuading him to let her do what he had been manipulating her into doing in the first place. Then she said in dismay, 'But could we get to London in time? If Felicity finds the receipt missing immediately after I have taken it, she will write to the bank and send the letter by the royal mail coach, and nothing is faster than that.'

'All you need to do,' he soothed, 'is to let me have the receipt for an afternoon. I will make a fair copy, which you will return instead of the original.'

A sharp stab of fear shot through Agnes's brain. A cynical voice in her mind pointed out he appeared to have thought of everything. But his lips found hers again, and she gladly shut out that nasty voice.

The marquess stopped outside Felicity's room and

then decided to wait until morning. It was too late to speak to her. But the sight of that amorous couple wrapped in each other's arms in the blackness of the night had roused and stirred his senses and brought old dreams and longings flooding back.

He raised his hand and knocked gently. He was about to turn away when the door was opened by Felicity. She was wearing a white nightgown trimmed at the throat and wrists with fine lace, and over it she wore a white silk wrapper lined and trimmed with swansdown. Her thick chestnut hair was brushed down on her shoulders. 'Come in,' she cried.

'I should not have come,' he said awkwardly. 'You had better leave the door open.'

'It is too cold to sit in a draft,' said Felicity, 'and no one is about this time of night.' He walked in, and she shut the door behind them.

'I was successful in finding out where the properties are, but nothing else,' he said. 'But perhaps there might be someone there who can tell us something about Mrs Waverley.'

Felicity knelt down on the hearth and picked up the tongs. 'I had better make up the fire,' she said. 'It has turned chilly.' He knelt down beside her and took the tongs away from her. 'Let me do that,' he said.

She smiled at him suddenly. He knelt there beside her and then gently put the tongs back on the hearth and turned to her. The candlelight was shining on her hair, and her eyes were large and dark. Her lashes were so long, he could see the shadow of them on her cheeks. He could smell the light flower perfume she wore. He put his hands lightly on her shoulders and bent his head toward her lips.

He felt her tremble slightly under his hands. He remembered his wife's disgust at any physical intimacy whatsoever. He could not bear any form of rejection from Felicity Waverley. That he realized with a stab of pain. He shook her shoulders lightly and said huskily, 'Go to bed. It's late. We'll talk in the morning.'

Felicity nodded dumbly but did not meet his gaze. He rose and left the room.

Felicity got shakily to her feet. She had been so sure he meant to kiss her. She had wanted him to kiss her. She clenched her hands into fists and glared bleakly about the room. How terrible to fall in love with the very man who might find out your birth was so disgraceful, he could not possibly marry you!

The marquess had hired a curricle to drive about the town. It also meant he could avoid taking Agnes along with them as he would have had to do if he and Felicity had been in a closed carriage.

It was perhaps unfortunate for the comte's plans that the marquess chose to be especially kind to Agnes at breakfast. He felt guilty about leaving her behind. She was, after all, related to him and had had a poor sort of life, filled with snubs and neglects. He smiled at her and asked solicitously after her health and apologized for the first time for the rigors of the journey. Agnes blossomed under all this attention and became convinced once more the marquess was enamored of her. She felt very powerful. Here she was,

Agnes Joust, with two handsome men competing for her favors. The comte had asked her to meet him that night on the esplanade and to give him the receipt. He had said it would be safer to make the substitution overnight instead of leaving it to the insecurity of a bare afternoon.

When Agnes was finally told she was again being left behind, she accepted it with good grace. Of course, dear Simon was anxious to get this tiresome business about Felicity over and done with. She gave him a conspiratorial smile of sympathy.

She planned to take her knitting downstairs. She would need, of course, to keep her eyes on her work. With such dangerous charms as she had been proved to have, she must watch she did not ensnare any other poor gentleman.

She would go to meet the comte that evening just the same. Perhaps she might even let him kiss her in farewell. It would be a touching scene, but she would tell him gently that her heart belonged to Simon. Perhaps he might be so distraught he might dash himself on the rocks below the esplanade. Agnes gave a delighted shudder. She would try to hush it up, but it would get into the newspapers somehow, that Agnes Joust, fiancée of the Marquess of Darkwater, had driven an attractive French aristocrat to his doom. Women would stare at her jealously and accuse her of being a Delilah, but Simon would proudly take her arm as they walked out and, with flashing eyes, defy anyone to say anything against her. She might even allow Felicity to come on a visit after they were married, and gently, as a married woman, point out to the spinster Felicity the folly of a lady learning too much. 'Brains should be left to the men,' she would say. 'You know I have always told you that, Felicity dear. Now, there is a nice young man coming to dinner tonight who would suit you very well. The curate. Not very handsome, but a lady in your position cannot look too high.'

Felicity dressed in one of her best outfits to go driving with the marquess. She wore a morning gown of apple blossom sarcenet with a high ruff and a large mantle of pale blue mohair in the form of a cloak. On her head was a yellow straw hat with a brim *à la Pamela*, ornamented with a broad plain blue ribbon.

She felt shy in the marquess's company and longed for a return of their old easy companionship.

As they walked from the hotel together, she heard an elderly voice calling, 'Miss Waverley! Miss Waverley!'

Felicity turned around as Mrs Crabtree came hurrying up to her. Felicity introduced her to the marquess. 'Such a little thing,' said Mrs Crabtree, 'but I thought it might interest you. That lady we were talking about the other night, you know, the one whose name I could not remember.'

'Yes,' said Felicity. 'What was it?'

'It came to me in the middle of the night. It was Bride. Yes, yes, her name was Mrs Bride.'

EIGHT

'You have had a shock,' said the marquess as he climbed in beside Felicity and picked up the reins. 'What was all that about?'

'Drive on,' said Felicity quietly, 'and I will tell you.' He flicked the reins, and the horses tossed their manes and set out along the esplanade at a brisk trot. They had gone a little way when he slowed their pace and then said, 'Now, what did she say that upset you so?'

'That was a Mrs Crabtree,' said Felicity. 'I met her last night. She and her companions were talking about an old scandal. The Prince of Wales came here as a young man. One of the local matrons set her cap at him. I asked if the lady's name had been Mrs Waverley, and Mrs Crabtree said no. She has just told me she remembers the name. It was Bride. Mrs Bride.'

'And what is the significance of that?'

'That was the surname we had at the orphanage, Fanny, Frederica, and I. Bride. Oh, do you think . . . ?'

'I do not think it possible that the now Prince Regent stayed long enough to father three girls in Scarborough, however long ago, without the scandal being generally known. The occasional by-blow can be hushed up, but not three of them.'

'So you think it might be a coincidence?'

'No, not exactly. It only adds to the mystery.'

He turned into Cliff Place East, a cul-de-sac. The buildings were three stories high and made of red brick, in good order, and with the steps well-scrubbed.

The houses were divided up into apartments. They rang bells and knocked at doors, but no one appeared to have heard of Mrs Waverley. The rent was collected by a man from the lawyer's office; that was all they knew.

'Is there anyone quite old living here?' asked the marquess. He was told there was an old lady called Mrs Shaw who lived in the attic at number seventeen.

It seemed a long climb up to the attic, and Felicity wondered how an old lady managed to cope with so many stairs.

Mrs Shaw answered the door herself. She was a dwarf of an old lady, with wisps of white hair escaping from under an enormous cap. Her face was criss-crossed with wrinkles, and she had ugly white hairs sprouting from her chin, but her faded gray eyes were sharp with intelligence. They introduced themselves and were ushered in, the marquess ducking his head to avoid bumping it on the low ceiling. The room was neat and clean, a clutter of odd bits of furniture, bric-a-brac, shawls and fans, and a linnet in a cage by the window.

The marquess explained they were trying to find out about a Mrs Waverley, and Mrs Shaw shook her head. 'I can remember everyone I ever met, and I never knew a Mrs Waverley,' she said.

'But she owns this property,' cried Felicity.

'Ah, but I never met or knew the owner of this property,' said Mrs Shaw. 'Someone in London, I believe.'

Felicity turned her head away to hide her disappointment. The marquess was just picking up his hat and gloves again to take his leave when Felicity suddenly said, 'But did you ever know a Mrs Bride?'

'Ah, her,' said Mrs Shaw with a cackle of laughter. 'What a woman!'

'Tell me about her,' said Felicity.

'She was a buxom, handsome lass who had just given birth to a baby girl. Her husband was a rich landowner. I think he owned coal mines in Durham, although they lived in York. They came here so Mrs Bride could drink the waters and recuperate after the birth. The Prince of Wales, a wild young man at that time, came here, and well, they barely tried to hide their love for each other.'

'Mrs Bride and the prince?'

'Yes.'

'And what happened?'

'Such a scandal it was,' said Mrs Shaw dreamily. 'Such excitement. And then all at once it was over. The Brides disappeared from Scarborough, and the prince's fancy was taken by someone else, quite a plain woman.'

'Do you know her name?'

'Let me see, it was a Lady Torry, a Scottish lady.'

'Do you know exactly where in York the Brides lived?'

'I could not say. No one here ever saw either of them again.'

'So we had better travel to York today,' said the marquess as they climbed into the carriage again. 'I am sure if we find out about the Brides, we will find out about Mrs Waverley.'

They were turning out of the cul-de-sac when Felicity thought she saw two people she recognized, but when she twisted about and looked back, there was no one there.

'That's odd,' she said. 'I thought I saw Comfrey and Harris. They were standing at the corner of the street. But I must be mistaken.'

'Just in case you are not mistaken,' he said grimly, 'we had better set out for York right away.'

Agnes was upset at the speed of their departure. She scribbled a hasty note to the comte to say she had gone to York and that Darkwater had sent a servant to reserve rooms for them at the Swan Inn. She felt for a moment she should tell him she could not see him again, but then the idea that a jealous suitor in hot pursuit might bring the marquess up to the mark occurred to her, so she sent him her love instead.

But she did wish she had told the comte to be careful in approaching her again, for the marquess's servants were all armed, pistols primed and ready, and Felicity was calmly sitting in the traveling carriage and priming her little pistol like a veteran.

'Why are you doing that?' cried Agnes. 'It is a sunny day, and we shall reach York by nightfall. There is no fear of highwaymen.'

'You never know,' was all Felicity would say.

'Are you any nearer in solving the mystery?' asked Agnes curiously.

'Perhaps. I do not know.'

'Poor Simon,' sighed Agnes. 'I am sure it is a burdensome task for him. I am sure he now wishes to wed and to return with his bride to the West Indies.'

Felicity carefully placed the loaded pistol on the seat beside her and said in a colorless voice, 'I did not know he was interested in any lady.'

Agnes gave a sly little giggle. 'I will not betray Simon's secret, but be assured, he is on the point of proposing marriage.'

'Why did he not tell me?' asked Felicity. 'I would have gone on with the investigation myself.'

'Well, it is not likely he would confide something of such an intimate nature to you,' said Agnes. 'I, being of his own blood, am a different matter.'

'And who *is* this lady?'

'I was told in confidence,' said Agnes primly.

Felicity felt very low. She had thought he had been on the point of kissing her last night. She must have been mistaken. Of course he had no interest in her. He had been friendly and charming, but he had shown not one sign of wishing their relationship to be anything more serious, and he had had ample opportunity to do so, had he wished.

The carriage jolted across the moors, the sun shone down, and Felicity felt more miserable than she could ever remember feeling in the whole of her life.

Then as they were traveling through a tract of deserted moorland, the horses suddenly reared and plunged. The carriage slewed across the road, and there came a hoarse cry of 'Stand and deliver!'

Agnes screamed and flung herself facedown on the floor. There came several sharp explosions. Felicity seized her pistol, let down the glass, and leaned out. The carriage dipped and swayed as the marquess and his coachman jumped down from the box. The grooms and outriders were standing around two men who were sitting on the ground, one nursing his leg and the other his arm.

Felicity opened the door and climbed down onto the road and went to join the marquess.

'Take off their masks,' ordered the marquess. The groom, John, stooped down and ripped off the masks. From behind them, Agnes's hysterical screams sounded from the carriage.

'Harris and Comfrey,' said Felicity.

'They are both lucky to be alive,' said the marquess. 'Go back to the carriage and keep that silly woman away while I question these men, Miss Felicity. Tell her they are highwaymen.'

Felicity reluctantly returned to the carriage. Agnes was writhing on the floor, letting out piercing screams for help.

'Now, now, Agnes,' said Felicity wearily. 'It is all over. Two highwaymen held us up, but the marquess or his servants wounded them.'

Outside on the road, the marquess leveled his pistol at Harris and Comfrey. 'One of you had better talk,' he said. 'I can put your masks back on and shoot you dead and say I thought you were the highwaymen you pretended to be.'

Harris cursed and clutched his wounded leg. 'It was a joke,' he said hoarsely. 'Did it for a wager.'

The marquess turned to John. 'Shoot him in the other leg, John,' he said. The groom raised his pistol and took aim.

'No,' screamed Comfrey. 'Leave Harris alone. I'll tell you. I don't know what it's about but a friend of Prinny's told us to stop you somehow and turn you back to London. He said there was a purse of gold in it for us. We didn't ask any questions.'

'Then hear this,' said the marquess. 'You may make your own way to the nearest doctor and get your wounds attended to and then I suggest you return to London as fast as possible and tell the Prince Regent or whoever of his courtiers employed you that I shall be coming to see the prince on my return, and if he does not want a scandal to break about his ears, he had better leave me alone. Do you understand?' Both men nodded dumbly.

Agnes could hardly believe it as the coach began to roll forward again. She tried to catch a glimpse of the highwaymen, but by the time she put her head out of the window, the coach had turned a bend in the road and they were lost to view.

'What is Simon about?' she asked. 'Why did he not keep a guard on them while he sent someone for the constable?'

'I do not know,' said Felicity, more shaken by Agnes's news that the marquess meant to marry than by the attempted attack. 'Please be quiet, Agnes, and stop asking questions. I have the headache.'

Agnes sat back sulkily. She had screamed her best, yet the marquess had not even put his head in at the door to see how she was. She was glad she had not given the comte his quittance.

They arrived among the narrow lanes and twisted and jumbled buildings of York as night was falling. The old Tudor houses overhung the street, cutting off what little light of the day was left.

The Swan Inn was near the Minster, a bustling, prosperous place. They were all hungry, having not stopped to dine on the road, and were soon seated in a private parlor to enjoy a late supper. The landlord apologized for the paucity of the fare while his waiters set down a meal that would not have disgraced the finest table in England. There was a first course of macaroni soup and boiled mackerel, followed by entrées of scallops of fowl and lobster pudding. The second course consisted of boiled leg of lamb and spinach, roast sirloin of beef and horseradish sauce, and the third course of roast hare and salad, soufflé of rice, cheesecakes, strawberry jam tartlets, and orange jelly.

Agnes forgot her love life and ate her way steadily through the meal. Her downfall came with the strawberry tartlets. Neither the marquess nor Felicity wanted any, so Agnes ate the whole plateful, and by the time the covers were removed and the port passed round, she was feeling decidedly ill. She said weakly to the marquess that she wished to retire to her room for a few moments and made her escape. Instead, she went to the outside privy and was very sick indeed, after which she felt quite refreshed, Agnes being quite accustomed to gorging herself and then being ill. She then went to her room to bathe her face and put a little rouge on her cheeks. Simon should not be left alone with Felicity for too long. So wearisome for the poor man. Felicity would no doubt be talking about crops or drainage or some such boring thing.

Just before she left, she glanced out her window, which overlooked the inn yard, and saw the Comte D'Angiers strolling across the cobbles. She half raised her hand and then backed away. He would expect her to take that receipt for the jewels. And why bother? Why ruin her chances of being a marchioness?

A silence fell between the marquess and Felicity after Agnes had left the room. At last he said gently, 'What is the matter? I know you have had a dreadful fright, but I am sure something else is troubling you.'

'I feel guilty,' said Felicity in a low voice.

'About what?'

'About you, my lord. You are chasing across the north of England on my affairs when you should be in London making preparations for your wedding.'

'I? What or who put such a silly idea in your head?'

'Agnes . . . Miss Joust . . . said you were about to marry.'

His lips tightened. 'Miss Joust becomes sillier and more wearisome by the minute. I have no intention of marrying anyone at the moment.'

'Oh.' Felicity knew she should feel relieved, but she continued to feel low in spirits. That 'no intention of marrying anyone' had done the damage.

She looked at him from under her lashes. He was leaning back in his chair, studying her face with a mixture of affection and amusement.

Felicity wished he would look at her in some different way, that he would show some sign of being attracted to her. Her head ached. She rose to her feet, and he rose as well. 'Excuse me, my lord,' she said. 'I must lie down.'

He stood aside to let her pass, and then his hand seemed to shoot out of its own volition to catch her by the arm. 'Felicity,' he said.

She looked up into his eyes. He was looking down at her warily, apprehensively.

How she found the courage to do it, how she instinctively knew she must do it, she never knew. But something made her put both her hands against his chest. He gently brushed a tendril of hair back from her face.

'Felicity,' he said again. His lips met hers in a cool, firm kiss, almost a boyish kiss. Felicity's body leapt into flame, her lips softening against his. He gave a muffled exclamation and held her closely, burying his mouth in hers, delighted and amazed at her answering

155

passion, moving his hands to caress her cheeks and then burying them in the thick tresses of her hair as his mouth explored hers and his lean hard body fused against the softness of her own. At the back of his brain, he felt he should say something, make some declaration of love, but he was frightened to break the spell. His whole world had narrowed down to this raftered inn room with the smells of wine and cooking, the smoky fire, the flower perfume she wore, the feel of her lips and skin, the ecstasy of that young body pulsing against his own.

Agnes softly opened the door and then stood, stricken.

They did not hear her. The marquess slowly gathered Felicity up in his arms and sat down, cradling her on his lap.

Agnes quietly closed the door again and leaned her back against it, her face flaming with mortification. She might have known it. Felicity Waverley was a slut! He would not marry her. He could not marry such as she. But while he was dallying with that tart, that wanton, that Felicity, he could not notice the pearl of womanhood that was Agnes Joust. She adjusted her shawl about her shoulders with shaking fingers and went downstairs and out into the courtyard of the inn and looked about. A black shadow moved in the blackness of the corner of the courtyard near the stables. She made her way toward it, calling softly, 'My dear comte! Is it really you?'

The marquess freed his lips at last and said softly against Felicity's hair, 'Do I frighten you?'

'No. Yes. Are you dallying with me because I am available?'

'You enchant me.'

He tenderly kissed her throat. 'Now I must leave you,' he said.

Felicity shivered, suddenly cold. 'Why? Where are you going?'

'To get a special license, my love.'

Felicity Waverley's hazel eyes blazed with love and relief. 'Oh, Simon,' she cried, and flung herself against his chest with such force that the chair toppled backward and spilled them both onto the floor. He rolled over on top of her and then kissed her lovingly and longingly, straining her to him.

He said at last, 'Do we need to go on with this business? Does it really matter who or what Mrs Waverley was? Or this Mrs Bride?'

Felicity sighed. 'Yes, it does. I have a feeling we are very close to the solution.'

'Then we will go ahead with it. But you must realize we will be married whether your parents turn out to be jailbirds or something equally horrible. I do not want you turning to me and renouncing me through some mistaken idea of honor.'

'I'll never let you go,' said Felicity.

'Then kiss me again.'

'Kiss me again, darling Agnes,' the comte was saying.

Agnes held back a little. Disappointment in the marquess was making her more inclined to be more suspicious than she would normally have been. 'Before I kiss you,' she said, 'when are we to be married?'

'As soon as we collect the jewels, light of my life.'

Agnes looked mutinous. 'If you loved me, you would get a special license and marry me now. Perhaps it is only the jewels you want.'

The comte thought quickly. He had been married twice before. What difference would a third make? And he could soon be shot of her once he had his hands on the Waverley jewels.

'I shall get a special license in the morning,' he said. 'Now kiss me.'

'Meet me on the steps of the Minster tomorrow at ten in the morning with the special license,' said Agnes, 'and then I will give you the receipt.'

Drugged and dizzy with kisses and caresses, Felicity stirred in the marquess's arms. 'I do not think we should tell Agnes,' she said softly. 'She is a little in love with you, I think.'

'I will put her on the London stage tomorrow!'

'But she has nowhere to go.'

'One of my aunts in Devon will, I think, accept Agnes as a guest until I find somewhere to settle her. I shall send her to London with a generous amount of money so she may stay at one of the best hotels before journeying on to Devon. She must go as soon as possible because I am going to marry you as soon as it can be arranged.'

'But does it not take two weeks to get a special license?'

'Not when so many of the clergy are in need of money. I shall marry you again in London. Will you come to the Indies with me?'

'Of course. I am very strong. You must not worry about me. It must have been a sad blow losing your wife. You never speak of her.'

'The marriage did not last very long. I . . . it was not really a marriage.'

'Why?'

They were now sitting in an armchair in front of the fire. He said against her hair, 'I frightened her. Physically. She would not have me in her bed. I do not want to frighten you or disgust you, Felicity, for if you rejected me, I could not bear it.'

Felicity took a deep breath. 'Come now, Simon. Come to my bedchamber and let us lay your ghosts.'

'After marriage, my brave girl. Kiss me again and then I shall go out in the streets of York to find a special license.'

But it took the marquess at least half an hour to tear himself away from more kisses and embraces.

Agnes heard the marquess returning at two in the morning. Her room was next to Felicity's. She opened her door a crack to make sure it was he. A dim lamp in the corridor showed her it was indeed the marquess, and he was knocking softly at Felicity's door.

As Agnes watched, Felicity opened the door. She was wearing a filmy nightgown with priceless lace at the neck and wrists. She stretched up and wound her arms around the marquess's neck and then she drew him into the room and closed the door behind them.

Slut! thought Agnes furiously. She dived into bed and put the pillow over her ears in case any disgraceful sounds of lovemaking should penetrate from the next room.

'I not only have a special license,' the marquess was saying, 'but I think I have found out where we can go to solve the mystery. The clergyman who gave me the license was quite old. He hemmed and hawed at the speed of the matter, but he needs money badly in order to feed the poor of his parish, and I paid him well. We fell to talking. He had never heard of anyone called Waverley, but he did remember a Mr Bride. He said the rector of St Edmund the King by the south gate of the city had a wealthy landowner called Bride among his parishioners and there was some dreadful scandal years ago. We shall go to this rector in the morning. Now I am going to leave you alone before I misbehave myself.'

He lifted her up and carried her to the bed and laid her gently down on it. He bent his head and kissed her tenderly. She pulled him down on top of her, and the bedsprings creaked, and next door Agnes bit the bolster in a fury and pulled the pillow more tightly about her ears.

At last, he disengaged himself. 'We will be married the day after tomorrow,' he said. 'We can wait till then.'

The marquess arose early the next morning and summoned Agnes to the private parlor. He looked tired but happy. Agnes thought he looked soiled.

'Your duties with us are finished, Miss Joust,' said the marquess. 'I have made arrangements for you to catch the royal mail coach at six this evening. I shall give you enough money to allow you to live at the best hotel in London for a week, and then I suggest you go to Aunt Tabitha's in Exbridge in Devon. She is kind, and you may stay there as her guest until I manage to make provision for you. I do not like to think of any relative of mine condemned to spend the rest of her days working as a companion. When I return to London, I shall see my lawyers and arrange for a settlement to be made on you. You will have a yearly pension and a sum of money as a dowry.'

Agnes stared at him with her mouth open. It was a generous offer. More than generous, although her vanity stopped her from realizing the marquess was possibly the only man in England kind enough to consider her to be still of a marriageable age. But the better side of her nature was soon silenced by her jealousy. She longed for revenge on Felicity, and what better revenge was there than taking away the Waverley jewels?

But she could not refuse to go. She would try to get the comte to travel on the mail coach with her.

She waited eagerly, hoping the marquess and Felicity would set out early so she could meet the comte at the Minster at ten o'clock.

To her relief, they set out at nine. She hurried to Felicity's bedchamber and found to her annoyance that the door was locked. But as she was known to be Felicity's companion, she was able to persuade the landlord to unlock the door with the spare key.

She went straight to Felicity's traveling desk, hoping that, too, would not prove to be locked. But she raised the lid easily and looked inside. She ignored the other papers as she scrabbled about, looking for the receipt. At last, she found it. She was arranging the other papers back in place when her eye fell on a letter from a London bookseller. In it, the bookseller was congratulating Felicity on the good sales of her first novel, *The Love Match*, and said he was looking forward to receiving her next manuscript.

Agnes was flooded with a heady feeling of triumph. Before she got on that mail coach, the marquess, dear Simon, should know Felicity Waverley had written that dreadful, that shocking, book.

When she met the comte on the steps of York Minster under the shadow of the great twin towers, she was by far the happier and livelier of the two. The comte had had no intention of paying any large sum of money to get a special license at short notice. He had become an expert forger and so he had been up all night forging the license. He held it out, and Agnes blushed and smiled and handed him the receipt for the jewels. 'But you must be quick,' she urged. 'Felicity has poisoned Simon's mind against me, and he is sending me off on the mail coach this evening at six. He says he will give me enough money to stay at a grand hotel in London before journeying to Aunt Tabitha in Devon.'

The comte thought quickly. He was staying in modest lodgings, but he had very little money left.

'I will not have time to book a seat on the mail coach myself, Agnes, my precious. Could you please secure a place for me, and I will reimburse you?'

Agnes readily agreed. 'Try to stop Miss Waverley or Darkwater from coming to see you off,' he added. 'I cannot conceal my love for you, and they might see it in my face. The bank receipt will be easily forged. I shall get it to you within the hour, and then we may look forward to our marriage.'

Agnes sighed romantically and agreed.

Felicity and the marquess walked with the rector in the walled garden of his home while the old man rambled on and digressed and then suddenly began to talk about Mr Bride. 'He was a very strict man. He was a printer at one time, and he gradually bought up land. He was called a landowner, but he did not own broad acres belonging to one estate. He had pieces of land here and property there and then coal was discovered on one of his pieces of land in Durham and then on another. He became very rich indeed. He married a young lady some fifteen years his junior in this very church. She was the daughter of a curate and had practically nothing in the way of a dowry. She had three daughters, one after the other, and after the birth of the last, he took her to Scarborough to recuperate, leaving the new baby and the other two with a nurse.

'He returned from Scarborough and came to see me. He was a broken man. He said his wife had had an affair with some highborn gentleman and he would never forgive her or speak to her again and he had turned her out in the streets. I cried out in vain against his cruelty. I begged him to make some provision for her. He said he did not want to be reminded of her. The next thing I heard, he had sent the children away. What became of Mrs Bride I shudder to think. People are very cruel.

'Then five years later he died. His will was published, and it was a great surprise. He left all his money to Mrs Bride. Whether the lawyers found her or not, I do not know.'

'But did Mrs Bride not return to her father?' asked the marquess.

'She tried. But her mother was dead and her father in ailing health. He would have nothing to do with her.'

'Have you ever heard of a Mrs Waverley?' asked Felicity.

'Let me see. I remember a Miss Waverley who was a close friend of Mrs Bride. She, too, was a curate's daughter and lived in a village outside York called Lower Demper.'

'Let us go to this Miss Waverley now,' urged Felicity after they had bade the rector good-bye.

'I think we should go tomorrow morning. I have made arrangements for us to be married at two tomorrow afternoon. Besides, we must say good-bye to Miss Joust. You may learn some sad news, Felicity. It is more than likely you are the daughters of poor Mrs Bride who was turned out in the streets to die. But if that is the case and Mrs Bride is indeed dead, then the Bride fortune belongs to you and your sisters.'

'I would rather find Mrs Bride alive,' said Felicity.

They went immediately to Agnes's room on their return. She was sitting waiting demurely, her bonnet on her head and her corded trunk at her feet. In her hand she held a letter, which she handed to the marquess. 'Read that,' she said, then sat back with her hands folded and a smile of triumph on her face.

'That's my letter!' cried Felicity, her face flaming. 'You have no right, no right at all, to read my correspondence.'

The marquess handed the letter to Felicity and said coldly to Agnes, 'Are you ready to leave?'

'But the letter!' cried Agnes, starting up. 'She wrote that book.'

'I knew Miss Felicity wrote that book long before I met her,' said the marquess. 'I thought she must be a very fast young lady. Then I discovered her racy knowledge came from a good grounding in the classics. I hope after we are married Felicity will continue to write.'

Agnes's nose turned bright red. 'Marry? You cannot marry her. She is a wanton.'

'Miss Joust, if you persist in insulting my future wife,' said the marquess evenly, 'I must withdraw my generous offer.'

There was nothing the now-frightened Agnes could do but beg Felicity's pardon. But her spite had had the effect of stopping either Felicity or the marquess from going to the mail coach to say good-bye to her. John, the groom, was sent instead.

Agnes climbed into the mail coach. The comte was

already there. She sat down beside him. 'We shall be married as soon as we reach London,' she said.

'Alas,' said the comte, 'the special license I got in York will not serve in London. We must wait a few days until I find another.'

'Give me the receipt for the jewels,' said Agnes, a sharp fear gripping her.

'There is no need, my love. I have it safe.'

'Give it to me,' said Agnes evenly, 'or I shall return to the inn and tell Darkwater what we have done.'

He reluctantly handed over the receipt, which Agnes popped down the front of her dress and wedged in the top of her corset.

The couple waited tensely as the clocks of York began to chime six o'clock.

'Will he never move?' cried the comte.

'Always waits for the Minster clock,' said a fat lady who had just climbed in.

Then there was a great boom from the Minster clock, the first stroke of six. The coachman cracked his whip, and the mail coach began to move off.

Agnes tried to remind herself she had nothing to fear, she would soon be married to this handsome man. But no rosy fantasy came to soothe her, only increasing dread that he meant to cheat her.

Miss Waverley, it transpired, ran the village school. She sent word to them that she refused to be disturbed until school was over. The marquess smiled at Felicity and said they may as well pass the time by getting married as planned. To Felicity, it was all a dream, the dark church, the hired witnesses, the brief service.

'I don't really feel married,' she said timidly as they left the church.

'It will grow on you,' he remarked cheerfully.

'I still cannot get over that you knew all along I had written that book,' said Felicity.

'I think I probably fell in love with you then,' said the marquess, 'when I saw you standing in that dark bookshop, clutching your manuscript. Now let us find out what this Miss Waverley has to say for herself.'

Miss Waverley ushered them into her home, a small cottage beside the school. She was a tall, thin lady with a mannish figure and a stern face.

Felicity explained that she suspected Mrs Bride might be her mother and wondered whether she was still alive.

Her heart beat hard as Miss Waverley replied, 'She is still alive.'

'Where may I find her?'

'I would like to write to her first and see whether she wants to see you,' said Miss Waverley. 'She does not reside near here. She lives in the south. If you give me your address in London, I will write to you there and let you know what she says.'

'And is she indeed my mother?' asked Felicity desperately.

'If you tell me a little of your history, Miss . . . ?'

'Lady Darkwater,' said the marquess. 'We are newly wed.'

Miss Waverley bowed from the waist. 'My felicitations, Lady Darkwater.'

'All I can remember is the orphanage,' said Felicity. 'The Pevensey orphanage. Fanny has some memory of another place before that, but not anything very clear. A Mrs Waverley came to the orphanage one day and adopted the three of us, Fanny, Frederica, and me. We lived with her in Hanover Square until she ran away to marry Baron Meldon. Tell me about Mrs Bride. We came looking for Mrs Waverley's past and found Mrs Bride's.'

'You know about the scandal?' asked Miss Waverley. Felicity nodded.

'She came to me, quite distraught. By that time, my parents were dead and I was even then running the school. She had always been a heedless, flighty thing, and I told her a woman with an uneducated mind had no resources. And so I proceeded to educate her. She had an agile mind and soon outstripped my knowledge. And then after five years, I read that Bride had died. I contacted his lawyers despite Mrs Bride's protests that he would have left her nothing. On the contrary, he had left her everything. I told her she now had her chance to build a school for young ladies and educate them as I had educated her. But the flighty part of her was still there. She said she was going to go to London to find her daughters. She settled a generous annuity on me, but I preferred to remain here and teach.'

Felicity looked at Miss Waverley's stern face and then said slowly. 'You do not need to write to my mother. I know who she is. She changed her name to

Waverley, did she not? She went to the orphanage and adopted her own daughters. Oh, why did she not tell us who she was? Why did she treat us so unnaturally, keeping us mewed up, playing tricks on us, setting us against one another?'

'It is her story,' said Miss Waverley harshly, 'and you must ask her her reasons.' She stood up to indicate the interview was at an end.

'I shall never forgive her. Never!' cried Felicity as they drove back to York.

'Then you will always wonder and wonder why she did it,' pointed out the marquess. 'The social column of the *Morning Post* today says both Lady Tredair and Lady Danger are back in London. There is an address for Fanny, Lady Tredair. Write to her and suggest the three of you to go to see Mrs Waverley.'

'Perhaps,' said Felicity. 'I should be relieved to find my parents were actually married and not criminals, but had they been, then they would have had an excuse for sending me to an orphanage.'

As he drove into the inn yard, he said, 'Do not look so downcast, my love. Remember we are married. Are you still worrying about Mrs Waverley?'

'No, Simon. I was wondering if losing my virginity was going to be very painful.'

'You have no doubt read extensively on the subject?' he said, half-exasperated, half-amused.

'Yes,' said Felicity, hanging her head.

'Well, my love, there is no need to rush into things. I can wait.' He helped her down from the carriage and tossed a coin to a hostler who had come running out.

He tucked her hand in his arm and led her toward the inn. 'I would not frighten you or hurt you for the world,' he said gently. 'You have had an upsetting day.'

Felicity frowned and worried all the way up to her room, remembering what he had said about his first wife.

At the door to her room, he kissed her gently on the forehead. 'I shall see you at dinner,' he said. 'I must speak to the landlord. We are late again.'

Felicity looked up at him, her eyes wide and dark. Then she turned and opened the door, then seized him by the hand and pulled him inside.

'What are you doing?' he asked, as she tore off her bonnet and pelisse and began to fumble with the tapes of her gown.

'I am getting into that bed with you,' said Mrs Waverley's daughter, 'before I change my mind.'

The York Minster clock boomed out the first stroke of midnight. Felicity lay with her head on her husband's naked chest. She awoke and rolled on top of him and luxuriously stretched against him, marveling how well their bodies fitted together.

He awoke, and his arms went tightly around her. 'What are you doing, my wanton?' he asked.

'Still trying to complete my education,' mumbled Felicity as his hands slid down to her bottom.

The next afternoon, Felicity sat at her writing desk and sleepily pulled a blank sheet of paper toward her. She began to write: 'Dear Fanny.' Then she frowned and tore up the paper, took a fresh sheet, and wrote: 'My very dear sister.'

At last she finished the letter and sanded it. She opened her desk to find a stick of sealing wax, when her eye fell on the bank receipt for the jewels. She picked it up and looked at it. Something was not quite right about it. The receipt, she remembered, had been in heavy black ink. But the ink now was a faded brown. The comte had not used the best ink for his forgery.

She stared at it. Agnes had been searching in this desk, which was how Agnes had found the bookseller's letter.

She picked it up and went through to her husband's room.

'Simon,' she said, 'do but look at this receipt. There is something odd about it. Do but mark the color of the ink. Then the bank manager, Mr Lombard, had an odd curly flourish at the end of the *d*.'

The marquess took out his quizzing glass and studied the document. He let out his breath in a long hiss. 'A forgery. Damn that long-nosed grasping bitch.'

'Can we let the bank know in time?'

He shook his head. 'She went by mail coach, and nothing is faster than that. She will probably go straight to the bank as soon as she arrives.'

'But they will surely not give her the jewels without a letter from me.'

'Whoever forged this for her, if she did not do it herself, will no doubt forge a suitable letter for her.'

'Then I am penniless . . . apart from the house in Hanover Square.'

He put his arms around her. 'After the riches you gave me last night, my sweeting, I do not care a damn about the Waverley jewels.'

'Are you sure?'

'Come to bed and I will show you how very sure I am.'

As he unfastened the tapes of her gown, Felicity said shyly, 'Do people make love all day and night like us?'

Her gown fell to the floor followed by her petticoat. He put his hands over her naked breasts and sighed against her hair. 'Who cares about what other people do. It is what we do to each other that matters. Damn Agnes Joust. The jewels will never bring her one fraction of the pleasure we enjoy.'

Agnes Joust followed the bank manager down to the vaults, her heart beating hard. At Limmer's Hotel, the comte was waiting for her return. He had given her a forged letter supposed to come from Felicity. He had tenderly kissed her goodbye and promised to marry her on the following morning.

But Agnes did not believe him. The part of her mind that had manufactured all those fantasies to trick her and comfort her did not seem to be able to work anymore. She now knew his hair was dyed. She knew his French accent was false. She knew she was afraid of him. On her way to the bank, she had torn up his forged letter. She presented herself to Mr Lombard, the manager, as Miss Waverley's companion and said Miss Waverley had instructed her to fetch a few items from the box. She looked a highly respectable lady, and she did have the receipt. The manager saw no reason to doubt her. Agnes felt sure if she only took some of the jewels and not all, Felicity would not trouble to report her to the authorities.

She had brought a large wash leather bag with her. Into it, she put the emerald necklace and bracelet. She would never sell *those.* Then a diamond parure, a sapphire brooch, a diamond tiara, twelve fine rings of various precious stones, and a collar of rubies.

She remained calm and ladylike until she was seated once more in the hired hack that had brought her, and then she burst into tears because nobody loved her and she was nothing more than a common thief.

She returned to the hotel where, unknown to the comte, she had packed her luggage early that morning and left it downstairs. She sweetly told the manager that she was leaving and that the Comte D'Angiers who was abovestairs would settle the bill. The hack was still waiting. She went straight to Rundell & Bridge, the famous jewelers, and, looking the very picture of respectability, sold the diamond parure for a very large sum of money indeed. Afterward she returned to the hack and continued on to the city, where she bought a seat on the mail coach for Dover. Napoleon no longer terrorized Europe, and she could travel freely. She endured the long miles of the journey in a frozen calm. She endured all the rigors of a rough crossing without complaint. She traveled in a foul stagecoach to Paris, barely noticing the discomfort. Once in Paris, she went to the best hotel, bespoke the best suite of rooms, telling the manager her lady's maid would be arriving shortly. Then she roused herself enough to go around the suite and turn all the pornographic pictures the French assumed the English visitors would adore to the wall. After that she lay on the silken cover of the bed and listened to the sounds of Paris.

And then all at once, that part of her mind that had seemed to be frozen for so long came back to life. Paris was full of handsome and dashing men. She would go downstairs to dine, and she would wear her lilac silk gown and the emeralds. *He* would approach her. 'I am smitten with your beauty,' he would say. He would be tall and blond and English. He would not be a mere marquess, but a duke. Agnes closed her eyes and smiled and followed the dream all the way back across the Channel to her triumphal wedding at Westminster Abbey, and was happy at last.

The Comte D'Angiers trudged along the Dover road, his boots cracked and his fine clothes covered with chalky dust. He had been wandering ever since his escape from the hotel. He did not know what had gone wrong. He had been so sure of Agnes, so very sure. He was wondering who he was going to pretend to be next. He would wait until nightfall and then stagger up the drive of some country home and say he had been attacked by highwaymen and his luggage and carriage stolen. He looked to right and left as he walked along, searching for a suitable mansion. Perhaps he should pretend to be a comte still. The ladies were his mark, and the ladies all had a soft spot for French aristocrats.

Then he saw a pair of imposing gateposts. He

stopped before he reached them. He did not want the lodgekeeper to see him. He climbed over the wall and slipped quietly into the green gloom of a small wood. He heard someone coming and lay down in a tangle of brush and brambles until he heard whoever it was go away. He would wait until dark, walk to the drive, then stagger up it and collapse artistically on the doorstep.

The owner of the mansion was a choleric squire with a passionate hatred for poachers. He stared wrathfully at his lodgekeeper. 'What d'ye mean, Jem . . . there's a ruffian on the grounds?'

'I marked him approaching the lodge,' said the lodgekeeper, 'but he never come past. Shabby individual. Must have climbed over the wall.'

'Get the gamekeepers out and tell them to shoot on sight this time. I'm wasting no more time in court.'

Night fell and a full moon rode above, silvering the landscape.

The comte rose stiffly from his hiding place, his bright blue coat grass-stained. He made his way cautiously toward the drive. He could not risk going to the gates in case the lodgekeeper refused him admission. He would say he had staggered over the wall after he had been beaten up by the highwaymen. He hoped there was some pretty lady in the house whose heart would be melted by his plight.

And then there was a flash of fire, and something struck him with a blow like a hammer in the chest. He cried out in sheer amazement, and as he fell dying to the ground, his last thought was that somehow it was all Agnes Joust's fault.

NINE

The three sisters sat in the drawing room of Baroness Meldon's home and awaited the arrival of their mother. The baron was visiting an old friend in a neighboring county, and his servants had not felt able to turn away three titled ladies from the gates.

The double doors to the drawing room were thrown open and Baroness Meldon, or Mrs Waverley, as she would always be to her daughters, walked in.

Her eyes ranged coldly from Fanny's golden beauty to Frederica's gypsyish looks to the slim elegance of Felicity.

'Why are you come?' she demanded harshly. 'I have no time for you.'

'Why not, *mother dear*?' demanded Felicity.

The baroness held onto a chair back for support. 'You know?' she whispered.

'Yes, we know,' flashed Frederica. 'But what we

do not know is why you should rescue us from that orphanage where we were placed through no fault of yours, yet not let us know we were your children.'

'But why must you know?' demanded the baroness passionately. 'You never cared for me, any of you. You have all married well. What do you want of me?'

'We demand an explanation, and we will stay here until we get it,' said Fanny in a cold, hard voice.

The baroness sat down and put her hands on her knees like a fisherwoman and glared at them. 'Very well. I hope I have trained your brains sufficiently so you will understand and not be shocked.

'I had just given birth to you, Felicity. It had been a hard labor, and the doctor advised Mr Bride to take me to Scarborough to take the waters. I had never been in love with your father. Does that surprise you? But my family had no money, and I was tired of being poor. I craved fine clothes and jewels and fun. My husband was a dour, withdrawn man, very religious. My life in York was dull and tedious.

'And then we went to Scarborough. Scarborough. What a magical place it seemed. All light and color and fine people and witty conversation. Then the Prince of Wales arrived with his entourage. I persuaded my husband to let me attend a ball that a certain Lady Torry was giving in the prince's honor. He saw me and asked me to dance – me, and nobody else. We fell madly in love. He was so beautiful then. We tried to be discreet, but word finally got to my husband. I told him I was going to live with the prince as his mistress. Then emissaries arrived from King George's court. I do not know what they said to the prince, but he refused to see me. My husband took me back to York. He said not a word on the journey, but when I got down from the carriage, he told the servants to keep me outside. He called me a harlot and told me to make my living on the streets. I went to my father, and he turned me away as well.

'I finally went to Miss Waverley, a schoolteacher. She told me I was suffering from neglecting my mind and education. She told me that men were beasts and fickle and only interested in women to satisfy their desires. I did not believe her.

'She lent me money, and I went back to Scarborough to see the prince. This time I did see him. He held me to him and kissed me and then he told me I must go away and never see him again. I asked him why. The pompous fool said I was causing a scandal and I owed it to England to leave him alone.'

She fell silent, and the girls waited. Then she began to speak again.

'The contempt I felt for him soon cured me of my infatuation. All my hate was reserved for Mr Bride. I learned through my spies that he had become slightly deranged and claimed you were probably not his daughters and so he had a nurse take you south and pay a foundling hospital to take you, and then he had you transferred to the orphanage. You were neither foundlings nor orphans, but then, money can take care of everything.

'When he died and left me all his money, it was like a miracle. I planned to take you out of the orphanage, and when the time was right, I would tell you I was really your mother.

'But there was no natural bond between us, no affection. I cried out for your love, and you spurned me.'

'That is not true,' said Frederica hotly. 'You would whisper wicked tales to one of us about the other so we were constantly quarreling, and when we found out what lies you were telling, we did not trust you. You could have had all our love had you told us the truth at the beginning.'

'How could I tell you the truth?' demanded the baroness. 'I did not want anyone to know Mrs Waverley was the once-scandalous Mrs Bride. I gave you love . . .'

'You fed us on a diet of constant emotional blackmail,' said Felicity. 'With all your knowledge and education, you should know nothing disaffects anyone more than that.'

The baroness shook her heavy head sadly. 'So ungrateful. So unkind. I am lucky to be married to a fine man. I shall try hard to forgive you, but I confess I have no liking left for any of you.'

'I suppose we should not have expected anything else,' said Fanny to Felicity and Frederica. She turned to her mother. 'Well, we thank you, Mother or Baroness or Mrs Waverley. I am sure I speak for all when I say that despite the lack of love on both sides, there is a home with one of us should you ever need us. Had it not been for your education, we might not all have been lucky enough to marry men who wanted us for ourselves alone.'

The three sisters rose to leave. 'Do you still have the jewels?' the baroness asked Felicity.

'All but a few items that were stolen from me,' said Felicity. 'I know the name of the thief, but my husband does not want to pursue her because of the scandal it would cause. Why do you ask? Do you want them back?'

'Yes,' said the baroness, fingering a heavy rope of pearls about her neck. 'I have only a few trinkets left.'

'Then you may have the lot,' said Felicity. 'I never want to see any of them again.'

'Come, let us not quarrel,' said the baroness, all smiles at last. 'You will deliver the jewels as soon as you can, Felicity, my chuck? Now we will take tea.'

'No, I thank you,' said Fanny. 'I feel we have spent too much time here already.'

'As you will,' said the baroness indifferently. 'But the jewels. I must have the jewels. I was a fool to leave them behind.'

'And what did you make of that?' demanded Felicity as they got back in their carriage.

'Strangely enough, she behaved exactly as I expected her to,' said Frederica. She put her arms around both her sisters and hugged them fiercely. 'We have found one another and that is all that matters.'

The baron arrived home that evening and said to his wife, 'The servants say three titled ladies called.'

'Oh, them,' said his wife. 'They were collecting for some charity. Do you remember, my love, that I left all the jewelry to Felicity?'

'Yes, and a damn silly thing to do, or so I thought at the time.'

'Well, the dear girl has written to me to say she is giving it all back to me. So sweet!'

'Don't wear it all at once,' said the baron. 'You used to look like a French ambassador's house during a victory celebration.'

'Always funning,' said his wife with a fond smile. 'Such a wit.'

'Yes, I know,' said the baron complacently. 'I always thought it was my wit that charmed the Prince Regent into giving me the title.'

The baroness's eyes narrowed a fraction. She was sure she knew why the prince had given him that title as she knew why she was somehow never allowed to go to London. But then she looked around at the comfort of her house and thought of her precious jewels soon to be returned to her.

'I am sure you are quite right, dear,' said the champion of women's rights. 'But then, you always are.'

The Marquess of Darkwater was finally ushered into the royal presence. He was not at all surprised to learn the prince had not yet gone to Brighton. He looked around the gathering of courtiers and said with a low bow, 'What I have to say to you, Sire, should not be overheard.'

The prince looked at him apprehensively, but he waved his fat hand, and the company filed out.

'Now, Darkwater,' said the prince sulkily, 'state your business.'

'I am come,' said the marquess, 'to tell you I know all about that affair you had in Scarborough years ago with a Mrs Bride, so there is no reason to set your bully boys on me again.'

'We don't know what you are talking about.'

'Yes, you do. Comfrey and Harris told me they had been set on me.'

The prince seemed to crumple. 'We have had enough of scandal,' he said. 'Our public hates us. We had to stop it.'

'But if Your Royal Highness had simply told me the truth,' said the marquess, 'I would have held my tongue. You had me believing the Waverley girls were your children.'

'Odd's fish, man!'

'And all it turns out to be is that a youthful fling of yours nearly ruined a woman's life. Why did you misbehave with a respectable Yorkshire matron? There are plenty of dashers at court to oblige you.'

'You would not think it to see her now,' said the prince mournfully, 'but she was so fresh and innocent and beautiful. Word got to the king. We could not do anything other than give her her quittance. You will not speak of this, Darkwater?'

'Not I, Sire. I only want your assurance that I and my wife will be left in peace.'

'Our word of honor.'

'Then I shall take my leave.'

'I loved her,' said the prince, dropping the royal 'we.' 'I loved her very much.'

The marquess sighed. This poor fat prince would

never love his wife because he fell hopelessly in love with quite unsuitable women – Mrs Fitzherbert being his current passion, a passion that showed no signs of dying.

He bowed his way out backward and, wheeling about, strode through the gilded, overheated rooms until he reached the fresh air outside. He was walking along Pall Mall when he found himself being hailed by Mr Fordyce.

'Darkwater,' cried Mr Fordyce. 'We are surely both the happiest of men. I read of your marriage to Felicity Waverley, and tomorrow you may read of my re-engagement to Lady Artemis.'

'I congratulate you, Fordyce. When is the wedding to be?'

'Almost immediately. My bride-to-be says she cannot wait.' He kissed his fingertips. 'Such fire! Such love! One day, she was all coldness and then the next, she was in my arms. Will you attend the wedding?'

'We should be delighted. We do not sail for the Indies for another month or two.'

'Lady Artemis has gone to call on Lady Felicity. Ah, if only I could hear what my darling is saying now, how she is describing her love for me.'

'So I had to promise to marry the fool,' Lady Artemis was saying. 'Faugh! Trapped like a rabbit.'

Felicity blushed slightly. 'But did you not consider, Lady Artemis, that . . . er . . . such a thing would happen?'

'Not I. I consulted some quack during my last

marriage and the idiot told me I should never breed. Children! I detest children. With all your knowledge, do you not know any way to get rid of the brat?'

Felicity wished Lady Artemis would leave and take her troubles with her. 'I do not suggest you answer any of the advertisements offering such a service,' she said. 'It is said the women only bleed to death or die of infection.'

Lady Artemis stood up and walked to the window. 'I suppose I shall have to go through with it and then farm the wretched baby out to some nurse. I declare! There is young Lord Western lately come to town. Such an Adonis! Such legs. He is talking to that frumpy Miss Nash. Fie, what a waste. I shall descend and see if I can make life difficult for her.'

After Lady Artemis had left, Felicity crossed to the window and looked down into Hanover Square. The handsome Lord Western had been leaning against the side of a vis-à-vis talking to a young lady and her mother. Lady Artemis sailed up, parasol twirling. She stopped and spoke. Lord Western laughed. Soon Lady Artemis and Lord Western were walking off round the square in the direction of her house.

Felicity shook her head. Poor Mr Fordyce. Did he deserve such a wife? And then Mrs Ricketts came in to say Caroline James had called.

Felicity's face lit up with pleasure, and she went to meet the actress with both hands outstretched in welcome.

'Tell me all your news,' said Caroline, who then listened as Felicity recounted her adventures.

'You do not need to worry about a plot for a book.' Caroline laughed. 'You have had so many adventures. Why do you still live here? Darkwater has his own house, has he not?'

'We are staying here to make preparations for our journey to the West Indies,' said Felicity. 'We have to find jobs for the female servants, except the inestimable Mrs Ricketts. Fanny and Frederica are quite jealous that I am to have her with me. She says she longs to see a country where the sun shines all day long. And what of you? And what of Mr Anderson?'

'We are to be married,' said Caroline. 'His mother has left town in disgust. I fought against it. He is so young, you know, but . . . I am very happy with him. Do you think I am doing wrong?'

'Not at all,' said Felicity. 'I shall dance at your wedding.'

Caroline took her leave, feeling elated and happy. No one in the theater seemed to consider her proposed marriage to Bernard odd, and Felicity seemed to think it was all right. She walked all the way to Covent Garden and mounted the stairs to her apartment. Bernard was lying on his stomach on the floor, drawing up sketches for yet another fantastic piece of stage machinery.

'You will make me jealous,' laughed Caroline. 'The manager says you attract more people than the actors.'

'Where did you go?' he asked anxiously. 'You were gone a long time.'

She knelt on the floor beside him and smoothed the hair from his brow. 'I went to see Felicity Waverley. She is now married to the Marquess of Darkwater. I told her we were to be married, and she was so delighted at the news, I felt happy and decided to walk home.'

He kissed her tenderly. 'You are always so sure someone will exclaim in horror at the idea. Now come and look at this design for a flying harlequin, and tell me it is the most wonderful thing you have ever seen.'

The Marquess of Darkwater arrived home in time to change for dinner. 'No Waverley sisters?' he teased. 'I was sure I would find Fanny or Frederica here. It is a wonder their husbands see anything of them at all.'

'It is marvelous to have a family,' said Felicity. They were standing in his bedroom, which he never slept in but only used as a changing room. He stripped off his shirt. 'Where is my valet, George? He is never around since we moved here.'

'He is the only male servant in a household full of female servants,' said Felicity. 'He lives like a king with housemaids running errands for him and Mrs Ricketts getting Cook to make treats for him. Shall I call him?'

'No, I'll dress myself. Kiss me first.'

She put her hands on his naked chest and smiled up into his eyes. He caught his breath, then held her close and kissed her fiercely. 'It's been so long,' he whispered at last.

'I know,' said Felicity. 'Since dawn this morning.'

His busy hands felt for the tapes of her gown, and his mouth came down on hers again.

Mary, the little housemaid, who had been posted at

the top of the stairs, listened hard. She heard the master's dressing room door opening and closing. Then there were sounds of footsteps, and her lady's bedroom door opened and closed. Mary listened harder until she heard a key clicking in the lock.

She ran down the stairs and into the servants' hall. 'Oh, mum,' she cried. 'They're at it again.'

'Watch that tongue of yours,' snapped Mrs Ricketts. 'Well, they won't be wanting any dinner, and it's a shame to waste it. Pass the lobster, Mr George, and pour the iced champagne, but see that Mary only gets half a glass because she does giggle so . . .'